WET WORK

The Landau Trilogy

Book Two

Burton Hersh

Tree Farm Books

COPYRIGHT APPLIED FOR

By Burton Hersh

Nonfiction
Edward Kennedy: An Intimate Biography (2010)
Bobby and J. Edgar (2007)
The Shadow President (1997)
The Old Boys (1992, 2002)
The Mellon Family (1978)
The Education of Edward Kennedy (1972)

Fiction
Wet Work (2017)
Comanche Country (2017)
The Hedge Fund (2013)
Nature of the Beast (2003)
Ski People (1967)

Copyright © 2017 Burton Hersh | Treefarm Books
All rights reserved.
U.S. Copyright Reistration Number: TXu 1-868-357
www.treefarmbooks.com
ISBN: 1546817441
ISBN-13: 978-1546817444

CHAPTER I

What shocks me now is how long it took to dope the whole thing out. Because I was there, early, while it was all coming together.

For me it started in D.C. that October. Admittedly I was preoccupied, keyed up from months of overwork and apprehensive as hell. Not long after 10 o'clock the following morning I was scheduled to mount my oral argument in front of all nine black-robed justices of the Supreme Court. The *U.S. Supreme Court*! Me, Michael Landau! My mouth went dry running through the talking points.

It had taken the best part of two years; we were ecstatic the previous May when we first got word that four of the Supremes OK'd our petition for review. The Florida courts had blockaded us all along; on short notice *Exhibitors Association vs. Florida* was at the top of the docket. Everything depended on me.

I had been going over my presentation in the hotel room all afternoon and broke it off to make my way down the street and meet up with Dad at dinner. It seemed to *me* I was prepared to justify every allegation in our brief, pound home the logic of my case, blanket every conclusion with precedents. I intended to go in unprotected – no notes. It was important as hell, everybody told me, to radiate self-assurance.

Except Dad, of course. "I'd try for pitiful," he recommended. "Maybe tremble as you round into your summation, stutter. The barefoot boy attorney from the Florida boondocks, on fire with idealism and maybe a little tongue-tied expounding civil liberties. Can you imagine how many puffed-up ganefs in tailored suits the so-called entertainment industry has paraded in front of these prima donnas to make the same case you're making?"

"It has a history," I had to admit. I was the lead attorney for the West Florida Association of Independent Film Exhibitors. I would be defending my clients' right to bring out a German film that had done a lot of business in Europe. Playing to the rednecks on the Christian Right, our oily Florida governor had sent his staties around to confiscate the prints after the first showing.

"And you don't think you're pushing the envelope?" Dad's strong, stubby fingers rotated the stem of his Martini glass provocatively. He was at Georgetown that fall, delivering the Perlemutter Lectures on Modern Economic Thought. Now he was testing my conviction. "What was that movie you're supposed to be defending?"

"Originally, *Mit Meiner Scheide Verteidige Ich Das Abendland.*"

Dad turned toward Saria, whom we had both just met. Saria was my Comanche wife Linda's half-sister, born into that scattered reservation family a matter of weeks after Linda's lawman father made an honest woman out of her half-breed mother, a bypassing social worker. Motivated from the start, Saria had ground through the University of Oklahoma College of Law and picked up an LL.M in Native American Affairs. A onetime classmate of Saria's groused to me afterwards that it was reverse discrimination that snagged her a clerkship with Supreme Court Justice Grover – "Lefty" – Stynehenge, who liked to rattle on about his Apache great-grandmother. Stynehenge was a throwback, the cantankerous old cowboy liberal on the bench.

"Provocative title, right?" Dad asked Saria.

"You got me— what language was that?" Saria was sipping Vermouth. She had that Indian way of hanging back in conversation, pupils all but lost beneath those deep epicanthic folds, obviously missing very little. Then suddenly she unloaded, coltish, capitalizing on that prairie drawl. From time to time she reached back gingerly as if to steady herself and straightened a comb sunk like a talisman in the heavy mounded clump of braids above her long neck.

Dad studied Saria for a moment. He was balding fast at this stage. The two Martinis he had already dispatched were reddening his massive scholar's forehead, his bulging, Slavic eyes were aglitter. "German. It's..the title is a little provocative."

I had never seen Dad back off like that before. "What it means," I told Saria, "is: 'With My Vagina I Will Defend The West.' It's a kind of a quasi-pornographic farce set in the Third Reich. Remember the propaganda films Leni Riefenstahl used to mill out for Hitler?"

"The Triumph of the Will!" Dad said. "What an epiphany! How our susceptible little Jewish hearts thrilled in Minneapolis when *that* showed up at the World Theater."

"I'm getting the needle," I explained to Saria. "Dad thinks that sort of stuff is trash. What we're all about is broadening the first amendment. The Court's been deadlocked since 1967 when Redrup vs. New York was published. Which meant, essentially, stay away from erections and penetration. That's not a lot of guidance. For our exhibitors."

"But chazerai like this has redeeming social value? Michael!" Dad loved to ride me when I took myself too seriously.

"It has its statement to make. A very energetic hooker shows up, and flashes the goods around, and *voila,* social betterment."

"I suppose," Dad said. He turned to Saria. "So -- what does your guy think? Or shouldn't I ask?"

Saria favored us with a wispy little smile. "Take it from me, professor, the secretaries here are *all over our butts* about what goes on in chambers. Don't ask, don't tell, you know? Especially individual cases."

"Sylvan, please. You're family."

"Everybody knows where Justice Stynehenge comes out on personal-liberty issues," Saria said. "Lefty is definitely – he's no-way hypocritical. He can be pissy. But never ever hypocritical."

"After five wives? He's got a lot to be straightforward about."

Saria crimped her lips at the corners. "Is Dad here always a panic like this?"

"You're looking at good behavior."

Saria let her eyes drift closed, then opened them again.
"This term comin' up already looks a wee bit hairy," Saria said. "You ought to see the docket. Mor'n a hundred cases. Then after the conference the Chief gets the word out he needs our written opinions overnight. Holdover liberal-types like Lefty, older members mostly, they get to grind away around the clock."

"How about the clerks?" I asked Saria.

"Not with any decision that amounts to anything, no way with our justice. You ought to follow him around in chambers, humpin' in and out on two canes. Arthritis is eating the old bugger up alive. He still intends to draft just about every word himself."

"Besides our all-important first-amendment breakthrough, what else is coming up?" I wondered.

"A lot of heavy-duty crud. The word is they'll probably get around to partial-birth abortion, finally. With all that fireworks in the newspapers about how left-wing authoritarianism is on the rise in Latin America, the rumor is the Court may get serious about the War Powers Resolution this term. Who gets to declare war. Before the troops go in."

"That would be a refreshing development," Dad said.

"They tell me Tea Party gunslingers are muttering about taking back responsibility for Congress. Revisit the Constitution. Nobody except the Chief Justice, or maybe some accountant at Halliburton, really wants a ball-buster like Iraq again. Although right his minute I'd betcha the Chief gonna pressure those three brain-dead toadies of his to stick with him. Lefty would *definitely* be the swing vote on that baby."

Dad looked up suddenly from his Cobb salad. "You actually think there's something in the works? I thought I saw an editorial last week in the *Journal*. Fuming over some kind of mutual-defense protocol involving Chavez in Venezuela and Nicaragua and Bolivia and Costa Rica. Particularly poisonous about that president of Costa Rica, Consuela something."

"Raposa," Saria said. "Consuela Raposa. Lefty goes on a lot about *her*, she inveigled ol' Lefty down there last year and gave him a medal." Saria checked the comb in her hair. "You got to hope they don't dick around with Costa Rica. I got there on a grant the summer after my first year in law school. It was a riot, a class-A democratic grab-it-in-the-dark party. Pura Vida, baby!"

Dad was reddening fast, on the edge of vehemence. "The crap the right is leaking to *The Wall Street Journal* is that all those Costa Rican socialists are reneging on discredited old trade agreements. Oil, gold, whatever. I heard some projection-of-power lunatic around the Vice President's Office is already beating the drum, this administration wants its own war. Go in fast under the radar and turn somebody upside down before the public catches on."

"That's what frosts Lefty," Saria said. "He says it always starts out like that, some pissy little skirmish, or whatever the president calls it. And then we get really involved. Then Congress papers it over with some kind of a resolution. Not really a declaration of war, but too late to pull out. "

"You've got *that* right." Dad rolled his eyes. "Where are those strict constructionists when we need them? A handful of helicopter support troops, and overnight, bang! Viet Nam. Jesus!"

Our table fell quiet. Beyond the plate-glass windows of our steak-house porch on Q. Street the horde of bureaucrats was thinning. Evening was settling in but it was stifling outside. Men still wearing neckties with their suitcoats flapping over their shoulders, half out of breath after hustling up Connecticut Avenue from the Dupont Circle Metro Station, headed toward the neighborhood's bowfront apartments along meticulously landscaped renovations. Bicycles, a leering black panhandler in a tee-shirt stenciled "Give To The Overendowed."

Dad was uncharacteristically silent. "My father served in Viet Nam," I said to Saria. "Those things stay with you."

Saria adjusted the comb in her hair. "We have a brother in the service," she volunteered. "Buffalo Hump."

I must have brightened up. "You mean Sonny. We certainly know him. He's helped out our side of the family more than—I can't really—"

"A hell of a lot," Dad put in. He was signaling me to shut up.

"Sonny is my half-brother," Saria said. "But he's better than a brother. He's awesome. Our father isn't – he tends to have....outside interests. When I wasn't away at the schools, Sonny brought me up." That wisp of a smile again. "When *he* wasn't away at schools. Valley Forge Military Academy! Where they dump maggots in the oatmeal."

"He told me about that," I said. Our little filets finally arrived.

"We don't eat that much meat," Saria said. "You go ahead take mine, I think the onion rings are going to be enough. I never was that crazy about red meat or anything. One time our father got clobbered and told me that my mother's name was Arapaho and all my kin were dog eaters. Crazy, what sticks in your head." She poured a lumpy stream of blue cheese dressing across the romaine lettuce in her salad and knocked back another Vermouth. "Did either of you know the justice has Indian blood?"

"Somebody told me that," I said.

"He maintains Apache, but look at how his eyes droop halfway to his cheekbones. I'd say it could be Navaho. Shoshone at the outside."

"That or old age," Dad said. "Time catches up with you."

"Maybe it's that rheumatoid arthritis." Saria hesitated. "The joke around chambers is how he glommed onto Hasna because she's so beefy and muscular. Before her it used to take a couple of flunkies to work those fancy cowboy boots onto those skinny little feet every morning. With her it's grab one ankle, push – it's on! We joke he married her to guarantee those painless injections."

"Lefty takes a lot of shots?"

"He lives on Bourbon and methotrexate pills. Embrel when it gets too bad, bang, right into the stomach muscles. That's how they met – Lefty can get abusive when he's drinking, and after a while that last woman gave up and moved out on him, took off for their camp in Florida. Hasna was a visiting nurse. We say she came around to give him an injection one time, and he ended up giving her one." Neither of us laughed. "Kind of a shitty story to put out there about Lefty," Saria acknowledged. "Robing Room humor."

The next day I pitched my argument to The Supremes, that choppy Areopagus. Surrounded by Doric columns, beneath a bas-relief featuring historic lawgivers from Moses to Confucius to Hammurabi to the slumping Napoleon in a snit after Waterloo, the nine justices stared down upon my presentation. Somberly. I thought at several points Lefty might fall asleep. Dad was watching, owlish, from the visitors' gallery.

I saw him fight a smirk when it was time for questions from the bench and one of the conservatives rumbled on and on enumerating the time-honored objections – pornography was a slippery slope, how do you hold the line when it came to what one of her more outspoken clerks refers to as "the consecrated limp dick standard"? When I cited Jacobellis vs. Ohio in re hard-core pornography, the Court's reigning strict constructionist shrugged and opened out his pudgy fingers and observed that *stare decisis* doth not transcend the Constitution.

I bobbed and weaved, returning at several moments to "evolving community tolerances." Europe was moving on, but we remained devoutly late-Victorian. Then there were considerations of art – great works that were forbidden at one stage turned out the masterpieces of their generation. What about Chaucer and de Sade?

Reporters from the D.C. papers covered it in the arts-and-entertainment pages and there was a feature in *The Tampa Bay Times*. I waited around Washington a couple of days, but when I called in one of the court officials told me it could be months before the opinion itself got handed down. If there were enough dissenters, that could amount to an opening for further consideration. Privacy issues and the effort to identify "contemporary community standards" required a great deal of jurisprudential agonizing.

There was allegedly a screening room in the basement of the courthouse where the justices were fond of running off footage like ours. There was one largely animated scene in our movie that involved a battalion of microscopic dwarfs with flackering torches and rampant pole axes storming our churning heroine's cervix. I would have liked to hear the liberals on the court identify the "redeeming social value" in that one.

CHAPTER II

What shocks me now is how long it took to dope the whole thing out. Because I was there, early, while it was all coming together. For me it started in D.C. that October. Admittedly I was preoccupied, keyed up from months of overwork and apprehensive as hell. Not long after 10 o'clock the following morning I was scheduled to mount my oral argument in front of all nine black-robed justices of the Supreme Court. The *U.S. Supreme Court*! Me, Michael Landau! My mouth went dry running through the talking points.

It had taken the best part of two years; we were ecstatic the previous May when we first got word that four of the Supremes OK'd our petition for review. The Florida courts had blockaded us all along; on short notice *Exhibitors Association vs. Florida* was at the top of the docket. Everything depended on me.

I had been going over my presentation in the hotel room all afternoon and broke it off to make my way down the street and meet up with Dad at dinner. It seemed to *me* I was prepared to justify every allegation in our brief, pound home the logic of my case, blanket every conclusion with precedents. I intended to go in unprotected – no notes. It was important as hell, everybody told me, to radiate self-assurance.

Except Dad, of course. "I'd try for pitiful," he recommended. "Maybe tremble as you round into your summation, stutter. The barefoot boy attorney from the Florida boondocks, on fire with idealism and maybe a little tongue-tied expounding civil liberties. Can you imagine how many puffed-up ganefs in tailored suits the so-called entertainment industry has paraded in front of these prima donnas to make the same case you're making?"

"It has a history," I had to admit. I was the lead attorney for the West Florida Association of Independent Film Exhibitors. I would be defending my clients' right to bring out a German film that had done a lot of business in Europe. Playing to the rednecks on the Christian Right, our oily Florida governor had sent his staties around to confiscate the prints after the first showing.

"And you don't think you're pushing the envelope?" Dad's strong, stubby fingers rotated the stem of his Martini glass provocatively. He was at Georgetown that fall, delivering the Perlemutter Lectures on Modern Economic Thought. Now he was testing my conviction. "What was that movie you're supposed to be defending?"

"Originally, *Mit Meiner Scheide Verteidige Ich Das Abendland.*"

Dad turned toward Saria, whom we had both just met. Saria was my Comanche wife Linda's half-sister, born into that scattered reservation family a matter of weeks after Linda's lawman father made an honest woman out of her half-breed mother, a bypassing social worker. Motivated from the start, Saria had ground through the University of Oklahoma College of Law and picked up an LL.M in Native American Affairs. A onetime classmate of Saria's groused to me afterwards that it was reverse discrimination that snagged her a clerkship with Supreme Court Justice Grover – "Lefty" – Stynehenge, who liked to rattle on about his Apache great-grandmother. Stynehenge was a throwback, the cantankerous old cowboy liberal on the bench.

"Provocative title, right?" Dad asked Saria.

"You got me— what language was that?" Saria was sipping Vermouth. She had that Indian way of hanging back in conversation, pupils all but lost beneath those deep epicanthic folds, obviously missing very little. Then suddenly she unloaded, coltish, capitalizing on that prairie drawl. From time to time she reached back gingerly as if to steady herself and straightened a comb sunk like a talisman in the heavy mounded clump of braids above her long neck.

Dad studied Saria for a moment. He was balding fast at this stage. The two Martinis he had already dispatched were reddening his massive scholar's forehead, his bulging, Slavic eyes were aglitter. "German. It's..the title is a little provocative."

I had never seen Dad back off like that before. "What it means," I told Saria, "is: 'With My Vagina I Will Defend The West.' It's a kind of a quasi-pornographic farce set in the Third Reich. Remember the propaganda films Leni Riefenstahl used to mill out for Hitler?"

"The Triumph of the Will!" Dad said. "What an epiphany! How our susceptible little Jewish hearts thrilled in Minneapolis when *that* showed up at the World

Theater."

"I'm getting the needle," I explained to Saria. "Dad thinks that sort of stuff is trash. What we're all about is broadening the first amendment. The Court's been deadlocked since 1967 when Redrup vs. New York was published. Which meant, essentially, stay away from erections and penetration. That's not a lot of guidance. For our exhibitors."

"But chazerai like this has redeeming social value? Michael!" Dad loved to ride me when I took myself too seriously.

"It has its statement to make. A very energetic hooker shows up, and flashes the goods around, and *voila,* social betterment."

"I suppose," Dad said. He turned to Saria. "So -- what does your guy think? Or shouldn't I ask?"

Saria favored us with a wispy little smile. "Take it from me, professor, the secretaries here are *all over our butts* about what goes on in chambers. Don't ask, don't tell, you know? Especially individual cases."

"Sylvan, please. You're family."

"Everybody knows where Justice Stynehenge comes out on personal-liberty issues," Saria said. "Lefty is definitely – he's no-way hypocritical. He can be pissy. But never ever hypocritical."

"After five wives? He's got a lot to be straightforward about."

Saria crimped her lips at the corners. "Is Dad here always a panic like this?"

"You're looking at good behavior."

Saria let her eyes drift closed, then opened them again.

"This term comin' up already looks a wee bit hairy," Saria said. "You ought to see the docket. Mor'n a hundred cases. Then after the conference the Chief gets the word out he needs our written opinions overnight. Holdover liberal-types like Lefty, older members mostly, they get to grind away around the clock."

"How about the clerks?" I asked Saria.

"Not with any decision that amounts to anything, no way with our justice. You ought to follow him around in chambers, humpin' in and out on two canes. Arthritis is eating the old bugger up alive. He still intends to draft just about every word himself."

"Besides our all-important first-amendment breakthrough, what else is coming up?" I wondered.

"A lot of heavy-duty crud. The word is they'll probably get around to partial-birth abortion, finally. With all that fireworks in the newspapers about how left-wing authoritarianism is on the rise in Latin America, the rumor is the Court may get serious about the War Powers Resolution this term. Who gets to declare war. Before the troops go in."

"That would be a refreshing development," Dad said.

"They tell me Tea Party gunslingers are muttering about taking back responsibility for Congress. Revisit the Constitution. Nobody except the Chief Justice, or maybe some accountant at Halliburton, really wants a ball-buster like Iraq again. Although right his minute I'd betcha the Chief gonna pressure those three brain-dead toadies of his to stick with him. Lefty would *definitely* be the swing vote on that baby."

Dad looked up suddenly from his Cobb salad. "You

actually think there's something in the works? I thought I saw an editorial last week in the *Journal*. Fuming over some kind of mutual-defense protocol involving Chavez in Venezuela and Nicaragua and Bolivia and Costa Rica. Particularly poisonous about that president of Costa Rica, Consuela something."

"Raposa," Saria said. "Consuela Raposa. Lefty goes on a lot about *her*, she inveigled ol' Lefty down there last year and gave him a medal." Saria checked the comb in her hair. "You got to hope they don't dick around with Costa Rica. I got there on a grant the summer after my first year in law school. It was a riot, a class-A democratic grab-it-in-the-dark party. Pura Vida, baby!"

Dad was reddening fast, on the edge of vehemence. "The crap the right is leaking to *The Wall Street Journal* is that all those Costa Rican socialists are reneging on discredited old trade agreements. Oil, gold, whatever. I heard some projection-of-power lunatic around the Vice President's Office is already beating the drum, this administration wants its own war. Go in fast under the radar and turn somebody upside down before the public catches on."

"That's what frosts Lefty," Saria said. "He says it always starts out like that, some pissy little skirmish, or whatever the president calls it. And then we get really involved. Then Congress papers it over with some kind of a resolution. Not really a declaration of war, but too late to pull out. "

"You've got *that* right." Dad rolled his eyes. "Where are those strict constructionists when we need them? A handful of helicopter support troops, and overnight, bang!

Viet Nam. Jesus!"

Our table fell quiet. Beyond the plate-glass windows of our steak-house porch on Q. Street the horde of bureaucrats was thinning. Evening was settling in but it was stifling outside. Men still wearing neckties with their suitcoats flapping over their shoulders, half out of breath after hustling up Connecticut Avenue from the Dupont Circle Metro Station, headed toward the neighborhood's bowfront apartments along meticulously landscaped renovations. Bicycles, a leering black panhandler in a tee-shirt stenciled "Give To The Overendowed."

Dad was uncharacteristically silent. "My father served in Viet Nam," I said to Saria. "Those things stay with you."

Saria adjusted the comb in her hair. "We have a brother in the service," she volunteered. "Buffalo Hump."

I must have brightened up. "You mean Sonny. We certainly know him. He's helped out our side of the family more than—I can't really—"

"A hell of a lot," Dad put in. He was signaling me to shut up.

"Sonny is my half-brother," Saria said. "But he's better than a brother. He's awesome. Our father isn't – he tends to have….outside interests. When I wasn't away at the schools, Sonny brought me up." That wisp of a smile again. "When *he* wasn't away at schools. Valley Forge Military Academy! Where they dump maggots in the oatmeal."

"He told me about that," I said. Our little filets finally arrived.

"We don't eat that much meat," Saria said. "You go

ahead take mine, I think the onion rings are going to be enough. I never was that crazy about red meat or anything. One time our father got clobbered and told me that my mother's name was Arapaho and all my kin were dog eaters. Crazy, what sticks in your head." She poured a lumpy stream of blue cheese dressing across the romaine lettuce in her salad and knocked back another Vermouth.

"Did either of you know the justice has Indian blood?"

"Somebody told me that," I said.

"He maintains Apache, but look at how his eyes droop halfway to his cheekbones. I'd say it could be Navaho. Shoshone at the outside."

"That or old age," Dad said. "Time catches up with you."

"Maybe it's that rheumatoid arthritis." Saria hesitated. "The joke around chambers is how he glommed onto Hasna because she's so beefy and muscular. Before her it used to take a couple of flunkies to work those fancy cowboy boots onto those skinny little feet every morning. With her it's grab one ankle, push – it's on! We joke he married her to guarantee those painless injections."

"Lefty takes a lot of shots?"

"He lives on Bourbon and methotrexate pills. Embrel when it gets too bad, bang, right into the stomach muscles. That's how they met – Lefty can get abusive when he's drinking, and after a while that last woman gave up and moved out on him, took off for their camp in Florida. Hasna was a visiting nurse. We say she came around to give him an injection one time, and he ended up giving her one." Neither of us laughed. "Kind of a shitty story to put out there about Lefty," Saria acknowledged. "Robing

Room humor."

The next day I pitched my argument to The Supremes, that choppy Areopagus. Surrounded by Doric columns, beneath a bas-relief featuring historic lawgivers from Moses to Confucius to Hammurabi to the slumping Napoleon in a snit after Waterloo, the nine justices stared down upon my presentation. Somberly. I thought at several points Lefty might fall asleep. Dad was watching, owlish, from the visitors' gallery.

I saw him fight a smirk when it was time for questions from the bench and one of the conservatives rumbled on and on enumerating the time-honored objections – pornography was a slippery slope, how do you hold the line when it came to what one of her more outspoken clerks refers to as "the consecrated limp dick standard"? When I cited Jacobellis vs. Ohio in re hard-core pornography, the Court's reigning strict constructionist shrugged and opened out his pudgy fingers and observed that *stare decisis* doth not transcend the Constitution.

I bobbed and weaved, returning at several moments to "evolving community tolerances." Europe was moving on, but we remained devoutly late-Victorian. Then there were considerations of art – great works that were forbidden at one stage turned out the masterpieces of their generation. What about Chaucer and de Sade?

Reporters from the D.C. papers covered it in the arts-and-entertainment pages and there was a feature in *The Tampa Bay Times*. I waited around Washington a couple of days, but when I called in one of the court officials told me it could be months before the opinion itself got handed down. If there were enough dissenters, that could amount to an opening for further consideration. Privacy issues and the effort to identify "contemporary community standards" required a great deal of jurisprudential agonizing.

There was allegedly a screening room in the basement of the courthouse where the justices were fond of running off footage like ours. There was one largely animated scene in our movie that involved a battalion of microscopic dwarfs with flackering torches and rampant pole axes storming our churning heroine's cervix. I would have liked to hear the liberals on the court identify the "redeeming social value" in that one.

CHAPTER III

The nation's promotional handouts bill Costa Rica as "The Switzerland of Central America," and an illuminated fresco in the airport outside San Jose states flatly – in English – that the visitor has just arrived in "The Happiest Country in the World." There have been wars and revolutions and putsches, but that was in the past. Today is for democracy. "Pura Vida," says another placard above a glassed-in arboretum. We live the pure life here, everybody respecting everybody else's responsibilities while gratifying what is human and natural.

Our understanding was that I would meet Sonny in the airport Cambio, where we could exchange some money. He would be flying in from Cartagena. For me it had been a long day of breathing reprocessed air on several aging airliners, punctuated by a frantic scramble along moving sidewalks and trams and escalators between far-flung traffic hubs in Atlanta.

Fortunately I had carried on, so after a detour through the Sanitaria I proceeded directly from the gate toward customs and on into the main lobby. I spotted Sonny's angular silhouette waiting near the entrance to the Cambio, off to one side of the tellers servicing the tourists.

"Keep your American money in your pocket," he suggested. "The downtown banks give better rates."

Sonny had already acquired a vehicle for us, a Nissan Armada. "Always the oversized ride," I commented. "Never anything inconspicuous, some kind of discreet sedan, maybe."

Sonny slid open the side panel and heaved in my bag. "Sometimes it turns out you need space, Mikey," Sonny said. "Opportunities come up. Always good to have a little extra carrying capacity."

"Like what? Were you intending to moonlight in the watermelon business?"

"That could be. Melons. Bodies. I know that in the movies they like to fold people into the trunks of cars. Out here in real life that can get iffy. People suffocate in places like that."

By then it was after seven in the evening. A mist was descending steadily as the dark settled. The highway into the downtown was packed, two lanes each way; big buildings with neon advertisements for auto agencies or American Express Tours overhung the hissing pavement as we crawled into town. It was the hour of the dog; I could already feel that universal Latin frenzy starting to unleash itself now that the working day was over.

"Now, what was all that about bodies?" I opened after a few minutes.

"That was to keep you interested. I realize you fight it, but I could see when you and I ran that game in Coral Gables that you have a lot of potential."

"What potential? I thought this week was entirely about fishing?"

"We'll do our fishing. I'm just coming down from a week in the foothills of the Andes spooking out the remnants of FARC. Our Defense Intelligence computer monkeys think they're on the move again. At my end this involved five days of crawling around in the jungle, which impacts the knees. I'm due for R and R. Bright lights."

"I thought you braves could run all day and all night and get by on bark you chewed off the trees."

"That was my father's generation. I got softened up in boot camp."

Sonny had booked rooms for us in the Gran Hotel Costa Rica. An Italianate showplace when it went up in the thirties, back behind a plaza of its own in the middle of the raucous downtown off the Central Boulevard Peatonal, the Gran Hotel was a labyrinth of Byzantine-tiled colonnades trimmed out in ebony paneling, meticulously staffed. But it was small. Air conditioning was spotty. The semicircle of benches that bordered the sweeping turnaround in front was littered with street people -- kissing, feeding, alternately teasing with crumbs and stomping away the swarm of pigeons. One tattered old derelict lay shoeless beneath a bench.

While Sonny arranged for the Armada I checked myself in. Sonny had made reservations for two separate rooms, on different floors. Before I could stop him a bellhop in the house tuxedo plucked up my bag and conducted me to my room on the fourth floor and presented my brass key.

The room was small but immaculate, complete to the

enormous white fan-tailed bath-towel fashioned into a preening swan in the middle of my bed. I lay down alongside it, unwilling to flap out something so impressive. The day was starting to tell on me.

I was half asleep when Sonny knocked. I think I grunted something. He let himself in and took the single chair.

"I'm in 571," Sonny said. "Up one floor." He was looking me over a little strangely, his long legs doubled up in front of him while, rather hesitantly, he passed one boney hand through his wiry blue-black semi-pompadour. I had the impression Sonny was about to blush.

"What's with this aw-shucks presentation?" I said.

"Can't fool you. I guess I'm embarrassed," Sonny said. He hauled himself to his feet and rolled open my bathroom door and twisted open the cold-water spigots in both the lavatory and the shower. Then he sat back down.

"Something just developed, and who knows who could be listening? The services generally monitor hotels. This is the thing: My honcho in Special Operations Command sent me an eyes-only yesterday on a secure channel. An embassy attache here spotted one of those special-operations meatballs from the Agency. This character is very big at making an appearance just before the roof falls in."

"And?"

"We need to know what's next."

"What's next where? Here? What about our fishing trip?"

"That will happen." Sonny was regarding me. "OK, we're all family, right? Consider yourself no longer on a need-to-know basis." Sonny's weathered, bladed face pushed in very close to mine. "People – people with clout, right? – are interested in changing the way the natives do business down here."

"What kind of people?" I had to strain to hear against the drumming of the shower. Suddenly I remembered the conversation in Washington.

"Business people. Industrialists. They're looking for an excuse to shake things up, dump La Presidenta Raposa and install some stooge who'd let them tear hell out of the place."

"But I don't see—"

"It's not that complicated. Costa Rica has some attractive gold deposits, which the Canadians were starting to strip-mine until the government here shut them down because they were bulldozing the tops off the hills. These days it's back to a cottage industry for the locals. Then there is that oil in the north just south of Nicaragua, but La Presidenta won't let our seismologists in. Lately there are rumors pointing to serious deposits of rhodium, without which the nuclear industries would probably close down. Guesswork, but the major corporations are out there gnashing their teeth. Unfortunately for the interests, environmentalists run the government..

"It happens that vice president Sheel is loaded up with Canadian mining stocks in his blind trust, and he has been reaching out to- to counterparts in the intelligence community to loosen things up around here."

"Like who?"

"The usual actors. Most people have figured out that CIA has been a collection agency for the corporations since the end of the forties. Blew up a democracy in Iran for BP and left Guatemala a hellhole for United Fruit in the fifties."

"So where do you fit in?"

"Our problem – the military's problem – is, the vice-president and his cronies are fond of backing the country into these face-offs, but it's the soldiers who wind up spilling blood. A lot of it never makes the papers. During the Reagan years people in the administration were dying to mix it up with Nicaragua. We sent a company of Marines in through the jungle to reconnoiter and not one tender young recruit came back. Misquito Indians with blowguns. We heard years later they ate the corpses. Central America is iffy. Our guys are hesitant to try that again."

"So this is jurisdictional?"

"That, certainly. Also – there are strategic considerations. Remember "Operation Just Cause" in Panama? Hundreds of our own get clobbered and three or four thousand of the locals wind up blown away to dislodge a drug dealer the Agency itself raised from a pup? The region is starting to get it together. We need a few friends down here."

"So fishing is off the agenda?"

"No. *No*." Sonny hunched deeply forward, four-square in my face. "Maybe we just add a couple of activities."

My stomach was tightening. "Did anybody ever tell you," I said slowly, "that you have extraordinarily beady eyes? How come I never picked up on that?"

"I get that all the time. In native-American circles a

strong gaze guarantees integrity. The Sioux say *wilasayatapika*, 'men that are talked about.' Big asset. Helps sell used cars." Neither of us laughed. "I could use a little backup with this," Sonny said finally.

"Great."

"I hate to bring this up. But who rode shotgun for the Landau fortune?"

"That was personal. This is geopolitical."

Sonny shrugged.

I exhaled slowly. "What have you got in mind? Will I be entitled to a military funeral?"

Sonny's thin lips lifted on one side. "Full honors. Arlington, maybe. I'll get right on the eulogy."

I got off the bed and went into the little bathroom and took a long, reflective leak. The water was pounding away, puddling slowly across the floor. When I got back Sonny was sitting on the corner of the bed. I settled into the chair.

"OK," I said. "What?"

"You're the convivial type," Sonny said. "How would you feel about making a new friend?"

"How many friends do I need? I've got you."

"This muchacho is different. Expand your range." I didn't say anything. "Remember I told you there was this meatball our people tell me is floating around San Jose right now? The guy that lights the fuse? He calls himself Stan – Staniford Clinton Murtha. I have the feeling he'd hit it off with you."

"Why me? You've got that magnetic gaze."

"Never happen with me. I've been in and out too much, I'm blown, in fact we shouldn't be seen together around the hotel. Besides which, Stan has social pretentions. He is actually a very light-skinned Mexican with aquiline features from Arizona who came into the Agency as a kid in the eighties during the Bill Casey maddog era. Technically, he was a political officer."

"How come he's still in business?"

"In his fifties? Knuckle-draggers like this guy aren't easy to find. Hard-core, no problems dropping lefties out of helicopters or slipping a lethal dose of LSD to a secretary who might be reading the boss's mail. Most of the covert types in the Agency today are what we redskins call blanket-asses. Too petrified to leave their compounds if they do get unlucky enough to catch an assignment anywhere near combat. Everything is Cover-Your-Ass, fuckers don't pick their noses without authorization. Then they submit an after-action report."

"So why is Murtha still in the Agency?"

"He isn't, I understand he's long since logged back on as a contractor with Specialty Services. Sort of a knockoff of Xe, what used to be Blackwater. Five times the pay, and a lot less oversight. These retreads are known to gravel the mandarins in the Agency, but who else can they bring in if it comes to wet work?"

"Which is?"

"Wet work? Straight from the KGB handbook. Means liquidating inconvenient people. Taking them out."

"Wonderful. And where do I come in?"

"Shouldn't be that hard. A few hours of brush-and-run. The book on Murtha is – he's a social climber. He started life as a Latino from Arizona, Generoso Sanchez, with maybe some Pima Indian. Now he's an Anglo. He's quite a boozer, and once you arrange to get next to him you keep on buying those drinks and pulling out those war stories."

"Maybe I don't—"

"You're a lawyer. Lead the witness. He loves to puff himself up, especially with gringos, and once he gets fried you won't be able to quiet him down. It'll just take stamina enough to stick with him whatever he has in mind until he passes out. At some stage he'll probably loosen up and give you some idea why he's in Costa Rica. Something we can think about doing something about."

"But how will I meet him?"

"That part is easy," Sonny said. "We know where he spends his evenings around here."

Before he left Sonny provided me a thin bundle of 10,000-colones notes, worth something like $200, and a schematic map of the downtown of San Jose. "Most of the livelier establishments like dollars," Sonny said. "Just count the change if you break any of the larger bills."

We were to meet in an hour and a half next to the bandstand in the Parque Morazan, a few blocks away. "We better not be seen together in the hotel," Sonny advised me. "The lobby here is closely watched. If you really have to come to my room, use the stairs. Lock up your passport in your luggage. Pickpockets. Passports fetch a premium."

"I'm enjoying this more every minute," I said. "A real family vacation."

"'Ahsk not what your country can do for you,'" Sonny said. "I know a place over in that neighborhood where we can get something to eat sort of on the fly."

CHAPTER IV

I turned the cold water in the sink off and cut back the shower. Oversplash was starting to saturate the bedroom rug. At that, I badly needed a shower myself. Once I had toweled off I set an alarm on my watch and all but passed out. The alarm waked me. I pulled on a jacket and an open shirt and took the stairs down and made my way out into the plaza. It was a lot of work remaining inconspicuous.

There were more street people sprawled around the benches. The mist had lifted and a Chihuahua had started yipping at the late-October moon, which was mostly full above the Teatro Nacional. The side-streets were thronged: street arabs peddling sun-glasses and Argentine cigarettes and off-brand chiclets, a corpulent old woman with an array of lottery tickets spread across a board on her lap. A windowless butcher shop with a display of carp and segmented blue fish that already smelled a little gone by. Couples clutched each other in door-wells above reeking garbage bags. Intoxicating, if in the Latin style: romance and dissolution.

Moments after I got to the park Sonny slid out from behind one of the pillars of the band-stand. A scrawny youngster, back arched, was attempting to juggle three neon batons while peddling a very shaky unicycle. Sonny tripped down the steps of the bandstand and dodged the youngster and led me out into the street and down a block into the Horsefeathers Casino.

The Casino was gloomy, crowded, nerve-jangling with the tape of a marimba band and the raucous excitement of perspiring men jamming the poker tables, barking out their raises for Texas Hold'em. Slots hammered along the walls, unbrokenly. There was a buffet. "The cracked crab here isn't bad at all," Sonny said. "I like the plantains and beans. Some kind of ribs, that looks like. Stay away from the pastries. These slap-happy Ticos think refrigeration is some kind of Nordamericano conspiracy to corrupt the environment. You can trust the beer."

"That's reassuring as hell. Any bobo sandwiches? I'd like to get that close to a fish before we pack it in."

We ate standing up. We both finished quickly and Sonny preceded me onto the street. I felt the one corona I had drunk, but still my heart had started to pound. Sonny led me into the tangle of back-streets. The foliage above us resonated to the screams of flocks of little green parrots. After a couple of minutes we seemed to be descending, signs indicated the Zoological Garden somewhere behind the trees.

"Your guy is in that hotel across the street," Sonny finally stopped to tell me; I was a little breathless. Three battered little lipstick-red taxis were stationed along the cracked, bumpy asphalt. At the top of a wide terra-cotta step, Sonny indicated a barred entrance like the main gate to a cell block. There was a push-button doorbell and a bronze plaque beside the lock headed *Hotel Casablanca.* "Historic location," Sonny said. "Simon Bolivar is supposed to have stopped off for a quickie. Some sleazeball from Morocco is the owner of record."

"That's reassuring. And Murtha's there now."

"He is there. While you were napping I ducked by. I got the feeling he's in for the night. Look for a heavy-set guy, not that tall, with kind of a flat guardsman's mustache and a canvas vest and shoot-me-first camo trousers. Your much-admired soldier-of-fortune look. This guy's a strutter. Here."

Sonny handed me a passport case. "Credentials. Besides the passport there are a couple of credit cards and something like a grand in each currency. You'll need money. Spend whatever you need to spend to keep your mark talking. Stick with the identity on the passport, Arnold vanden Heuvel. I told you, Murtha is a snob. The passport photo came from a cell-phone shot of you I took at your wedding. You looked very surprised and a little stricken, which is perfect for a passport."

"You side-winding son-of-a-bitch. You've been setting me up!"

"No more than was necessary. In this game, preparation counts for a lot. Which reminds me." Sonny checked his pockets and came up with a couple of condoms. "You better keep these handy. Murtha likes the ladies."

"Great. Jesus. Where does patriotism end? You're sure you're not feeding *me* to him?"

"Probably not."

"You get to explain this whole goddamned travesty to

Linda."

"Me? Hey, what do the palefaces say: Whatever goes down in San Jose stays down in San Jose. Anyhow, you're the lawyer. Just watch those exchanges of bodily fluids."

"That's a help."

"When you can get away, take a taxi to the Teatro Nacional and find your way back to the hotel on the crowd. Please make sure nobody is on your tail."

"What else. Should I shoot somebody?"

"Hey, you're the gun nut in the group. I'm the pacifist."

I started across the street. I looked back once, but Sonny was gone.

Just as I started to ring the bell one of the cab-drivers accosted me, a small older man. "Senor," he proposed, resting a hand on my sleeve, "es posibilidad you like Viagra now? Cialis?" He had a disturbingly sweet smile. He opened one grimy palm on several blue pills and one peach-colored.

"I don't think so," I said.

"No?"

"No."

"Very good price," he said.

"Really, no."

He looked at me with something like compassion. "OK," he said. "Pura vida."

We touched fists just as the barred door swung out, then a paneled door inside. A tall fellow in a worn black pebbled-leather vest with very pouchy eyes and a single crimped lock of gray hair thrown back across his bare skull was looking me over. He removed the stub of his cigarette. "Here we have a club," he told me in not much more than a whisper. He pronounced it kloop, like a German.

"Ah." He was waiting. "What if I would like to join?"

"Why not? Ten thousand colones."

I pushed the bill on him and he let me into his hotel. There was a vaulting ante-room which did have the feel and congeniality of a shooting lodge in the post-colonial world. High on one wall were mounted the stuffed heads of four massive ruminants. The top three were a lugubrious water buffalo, an antelope with supercilious glass eyes, and an ibex with a long snout and wide, corkscrewed horns. Below – obviously the Alpha Male in the group – glowered the forward half of an enormous ward hog, all tusks and bristling, even in death.

"Impressive wall," I said.

"Shot by our owner, all four from them," the tall man said. "Madame al-Aziz."

There was a plaque beneath the wart hog's big bell of chest hair. Into the plaque had been carved: "I LOST MY VIRGINITY HERE, BUT I STILL HAVE THE BOX IT CAME IN!"

"Does that pertain to Madame al-Aziz too?" I was still feeling the corona.

The tall man straightened up, drew back. "Das ist ja *un*verschaemt," he hissed at me. "Madame al-Aziz is part of the highest circles. She is a descendant of the sultan."

"I lost my sense of proportion. Too many animal heads. Maybe I need a drink."

I sensed the tall man's skepticism, but he relented enough to lead me up a flight of stairs and nodded his permission for me to take a stool before the long mahogany bar. Two stools down, slumped over what looked like a whisky and water, was Staniford Clinton Murtha. The mustache was the tipoff. He had the face of a drinker: a shapeless nose reddened around the tip, as well as a network of exploded capillaries across Murtha's swollen cheeks.

Behind him, down a couple of steps and arrayed on a long L-shaped bench on a kind of mezzanine, were perhaps a dozen women. Most of them were short but appealing, with powerful hind-quarters. Several were grooming one another, tweezing out eyebrow bristles or styling each other's hair. One was painting the toenails of another girl in Grecian sandals a phosphorescent magenta.

I ordered a Margarita, which got Murtha's attention immediately. "You U.S.?" he looked up to ask.

"You bet," I said.

"Leave the mixed drinks alone. You wind up with a couple drops of triple sec and a hellova lot of lime juice. And water. No tequila. Then they load you up with crushed ice and that's it. People here are crushed-ice crazy. They dump it in the urinals every couple of hours. Supposed to keep the stink down. Loco, fucking loco!"

"Thanks," I said. "So, what do you do?"

"Me? Oh, you mean about drinking? I bring my own bottle and I make very damn sure the cocksuckers open it in front of me."

In front of a massive plasma screen on which a fast-moving soccer game was rousing some distant crowd, a fetching little Eurasian bartender was regarding Murtha through huge, well-charcoaled eyes. Her halter was loose, inviting further examination. "I didn't mean you, sugar," Murtha assured her. "I mean the other cocksuckers. How about you turn the sound down on the TV there?"

Murtha tossed me a heavy wink. "I bet you're wondering, is this loose cannon in the diplomatic service? Just kiddin' around. She knows me, don't you, baby? They're very forgiving, Tico pussy, around this town. As long as you tip em'."

Murtha took a swallow. "Patricia, sugar, why don't you give my pal here a real drink? Out of my bottle. What was that name again? You probably told me, but you know how it is."

"Arnold." I had to take a breath. "Arnold vanden Heuvel."

"No shit? Why do I think I know that name? I knew a broad in college. Put out like a rabbit with psoriasis, but was she way over on the left."

"What happened?"

"Who knows? I think she might have died, or went into publishing or some damn thing. In my business, Arnold—"

"Arnie. People call me Arnie."

"Whatever. In my business, people come and go so fucking fast you never really get to know anybody. I mean – anybody important. With stature."

"What business are you in?" I asked, lightly. My real drink arrived.

"My business? I'm in consulting. I'm a facilitator, a problem solver. My trouble is, I'm so goddamned successful I'm never anyplace long enough to make any contacts you'd want to follow up on." Murtha looked up. "

And how about me?" Murtha chided the bartender. "You're not going to freshen *my* drink?"

When that drink arrived Murtha craned around and surveyed the women below. "Good crop tonight, Arnie," he assured me. "When they bunch together like that you can smell twat from up here. "

There was a new arrival, a tall girl with GIVE stenciled onto her T-shirt and a gardenia in her hair. She slammed through behind the drinkers and hoisted her T-shirt to wag her nipples at the crowd on the bench. All her colleagues rose and received, one by one, lingering kisses on the lips.

"Like one big family," Murtha said. "Of perverts. How can anybody not love 'em all? I'm gonna hate to leave."

"You're going somewhere?"

"I'm headed north in two days. Cordillera de Tilaran, the fucked-out remains of the Gold Belt. One of my clients is all over me about a little dustup in the hills up there. You got your labor laws here—nobody can do business with all the fucking regulations they slap on foreigners. They watch every move outside investors make around here, fucking commie society. Somebody needs to loosen the bastards up."

"What you're saying is, the natives are restless?"

"Maybe not restless enough, if you catch my meaning."

"How you going to change that? You must have a hellova lot of influence."

"Thas all I'm gonna say," Murtha said. He was obviously feeling his whisky. "I told you, lotta people think I'm like their fairy godmother. Wave my wand.

Make everybody's dreams come true. Except after that you never even get a fucking thank-you or anything. Maybe – y'know – a Christmas card would be nice?"

Murtha was starting to sweat. The dye in what there was of his thinning hair was creeping onto his brow. Suddenly he was staring, without much comprehension, at nothing. Ernest Hemingway once wrote about a man with the eyes of an unsuccessful rapist; I knew then what that meant.

A big, short Levantine woman in a silk dress with half-a-dozen strands of pearls waddled up the several steps from below, followed by the tall man. Murtha gripped her shoulder as she attempted to pass. "You gotta meet my buddy here," Murtha husked out.

"The princess will be leaving for a few hours now," the tall man said.

"You gotta meet Professor vanden Heuvel," Murtha said. "Arnie. Arnold." Murtha patted the gray-shot lozenges of his heavy mustache. "Un celebridad muy grande. Rides to the hounds, old, old money."

Madame al-Aziz took my hand. She was so old and fat you almost couldn't see her eyes. "El gusto es mio."

"Arnie thinks you got on your hands here the hottest little cookie jar this side of Cairo, Egypt," Murtha said. "Arnie, is it true? Are you the son of the Terminator?"

"You might say that," I said. I was well along.

"What have you got around here that's really new and really different?" Murtha wanted to know. "Maybe a specialty act, something a world traveler like Arnie here might get something out of."

Suddenly Madame al-Aziz looked interested: She

concentrated her wrinkles. "Maybe the Doloroso Sisters? A lot of money, but if you like them both...."

Murtha spat. "To a vanden Heuvel? Money is insignificant."

"Five hundred thousand colones."

"Too rich for my blood," Murtha said. "That's what, like maybe a grand?"

"I could handle that," I said, before I could stop to think. What had Sonny said, do whatever you need to do? I felt the whisky in every cell.

"But that's for both of us," Murtha wanted to establish.

"We're having an American evening out," I heard myself babble. "Mi puta es su puta. My Spanish is definitely compromised, but you get what I'm saying."

The tall man explained that the Doloroso sisters lived in a flat somewhere in the neighborhood of the Hospital San Juan de Dios, behind the Mercado. They would be arriving in about twenty minutes. The management must insist on two hundred thousand colones now, and three hundred thousand after the performance, bitte. Would we please enjoy a Weltklass Cuban cigar compliments of the Hotel Casablanca. An authentic Hobima. Viel Vergnuegen.

I peeled the bills off, and we accepted the cigars. I never really smoked, but this promised to become a night to remember – if I lived through it. The tall man snipped the conical end off the cigars and lit them for both of us with his antique Ronson lighter. He started a fresh cigarette for himself.

"We model this place after the hunting lodge the

princess and her consort frequented in the early days," the tall man said. "In Kenya. When the British was present. Before the Mau Mau and those terrorists give it back to the Untermenschen. She frequented Kenya very much."

I took another puff on my cigar. It was certainly mellow. Murtha's whisky was a little raw, and the cigar was a help with that. The women seemed restless. One of them caught my eye and smiled and joined our party. The neckline of her blouse was provocatively low; a dusting of sparklers made her eyelids glisten. She stood very close to my face and very slowly and very sensuously applied lip gloss with a tiny brush. Her perfume made my nostrils flare: jasmine, astringent with emerging sweat. I handed her my cigar and she attempted a puff, languorously, puckering out those glossy lips.

The tall man hooked a thumb into his leather vest and spoke without reprimand: Na, na, Bonita, die Herren son ocupado. They await the Doloroso sisters."

Bonita straightened up, alarmed, as if from an unexpected shock. Slumping, she trudged back down to her bullpen of woman.

The Doloroso sisters arrived a minute or two later. The tall man introduced us. The rather stately woman with all the coal-black hair rippling down her back assertively swinging a giant handbag was the older sister. The sister with her hair up was shorter, rather lightly built, heavily made up. Murtha and I slid to our feet and the arrivals embraced us, formally.

Murtha demanded his bottle and four glasses and a carafe of water and ice. The bartender Patricia loaded all that along with a magnum of Champagne and four tulip glasses onto a tray and led our party into the back down a short, dusty corridor. This was an event at the Hotel Morocco, a séance involving the Doloroso sisters. Patricia unlocked a door at the end and we followed her into a dark apartment. She put the drinks down on the drop-leaf side table and turned on a couple of floor-lamps with streaky parchment shades and an emerald-glass torchiere. Fighting the suggestion of a smirk, Patricia eased back out into the corridor.

The taller sister pulled her handbag open and set out a battery-powered disc player on the end table in front of the mildewed burgundy drapes, which were pulled closed. "Isabella," she said, and tilted up her chin to regard us over milky cheekbones. She clasped her little sister's shoulder. "Rosa." Rosa jerked away: impudent, her own creature.

Isabella prodded the disc player and very rich percussive music filled the shadowy room. "Perfidia," Isabella explained. "With steel guitar." She stepped across to pour Champagne for everybody. We chinked glasses. Everybody drank. "Prepararse," Isabella said.

"Your arse or my arse," Murtha wanted to know.

Neither of them got the joke. Isabella hoisted her handbag and she and her sister flounced into the bathroom.

"What's next?" I asked Murtha. We stowed our cigars.

"You're out of uniform, man. Time for our fucking suits." Murtha's canvas vest was already off, followed by his camos and his underwear and his Doc Marten lowcuts. I began to disrobe. When I looked up Murtha was starkers: a sagging, pot-bellied veteran utterly bareass except for his webbed belt from which dangled a holster with its crosshatched 9 millimeter pistol butt bobbing against the crack of his ass. His dick looked stubby, harmless, the bulb virtually purple. I was just climbing out of my underwear. "Better get a move on, my short-peckered friend," Murtha advised. "And ditch the wedding ring. Even hookers like to fantasize."

A toilet flushed and the sisters made their entrance. Both were lightly wrapped in semi-diaphanous veils. "I think we must dance a little," Isabella said. "Bailar." She poured two fresh Champagnes and handed one glass to me. Her CD of Golden Oldies had just started on a bossa-nova track with *The Girl From Ipanema*. Isabella slid in against me. Her stomach felt very warm. Every fourth or fifth beat she arranged to bump her mound of Venus against me in time with the rich Samba rhythms. Her veil was starting to come open. I couldn't resist exploring. She was already wet, fluffy.

Murtha attempted to dance, but he was so much bigger than Rosa that her head kept butting him in the chest. He really couldn't dance in any case. After a few turns Murtha suddenly deposited himself, heavily, into one of the badly-worn Morris chairs and pulled Rosa in on top of him. She sat there on his knee, stony-faced, her makeup starting to powder away.

Murtha picked at the clasp that secured her veil just below one armpit and unwrapped her slowly, like a delicacy. Rosa's pale little cup-cake breasts came into view. Murtha squeezed her belly and opened her legs a little. He laid a forefinger on her pinched-up cleft. "We think we're sophisticated as hell, but these women could teach our ladies a thing or two," Murtha said. "This little honey's cunt feels hairless as a baby's to me."

Isabella stopped dancing. "These days we teach them to pull the hairs out," she said. "Better than to shave." The steel band moved on to slower music, *Besame Mucho.* Isabella gripped my butt with both hands and ground on me. She had already wound both her veils off and was slapping my chest playfully with her mature tits. "Like weapons," she breathed. "Big knockers."

"It's like the Junior-Senior prom," I said. "Anything goes. It's OK to get your water hot in front of the elders of the tribe."

"My water is gettin' hot, all right," Murtha said. Over Isabella's shoulder I saw how he had guided Rosa's little hand into tugging knowingly at his semi-erect penis. There was a lot of mischief in her little face. "Easy, baby," he told her after a few seconds. "One wrong move and we'll be digging five-millimeter slugs out of everybody's fanny. Arnold here don't want no bullet wounds to explain around the steam room of the Myopia Hunt Club or wherever. Where is that, Arnold? The Hamptons? Jupiter Island? See, I know the names at least."

I had a hard-on so intense I think it was draining most of the blood from what was left of my numb brain. "Bar Harbor," I muttered. "In the summers."

Murtha lapped down the last of his whisky and water. "Jesus Mother of God don't let this end," he said. "I figured I at least get to spend the week here, but now this afternoon I find out they want me in the sorry-ass field the day after tomorrow. Go kill the rest of this week nosing around the saddest jerkoff real estate in this entire humping country. Not even on most of the maps we use. Juntas. Someplace near the ass end of Abangares! Fucking slag

heap, most of it. Abandoned mines. "
"I never heard of it."
"And why? Because those candyasses at Langley sent in two pipsqueaks who obviously can't cut the mustard, and what comes back is: they ain't getttin' no-place. Fresh off the Farm. We need to raise a little dust down here, maybe a little bang-bang/boom-boom. Make some of these peacenik bureaucrats panic, get the local business community behind us. Overreact. Buy us some friends. They can't get nobody to listen."

"It's hard to find good people," I said. "We have that problem in every one of our companies."

"So you know what I'm getting' at. Easy, little lady. You're supposed to tune it up, not tear it off."

Isabella wanted to dance, not listen to us. A slightly syncopated version of that old Frank Sinatra favorite *My Way* was slowing us almost to a stand-still. Isabella cradled my balls and started to kiss me in one ear.

I danced Isabella over to Murtha's chair. Rosa had been rubbing her face against Murtha's shoulder while she fondled him. She looked up. I looked down. Most of her makeup had worn away. Her hair had worked loose of its pins.

"That's OK," Murtha said as Rosa dug deeper. He exhaled heavily. "I don't mind that." He looked up. "I had a wife once told me I had the testicles of a prince."

"Which prince was that?" I was giddy. "Does *he* know?"

"No, it's the truth, man, don't laugh. Shit, I never fucked a woman yet didn't come back for seconds."

Rose was scrounging deeper; abruptly Murtha's torso

heaved up halfway out of his chair. "For God's sake, you little bitch, what the hell was *that*? Jesus, that *hurt*!" Grabbing his gun belt behind him, Murtha reached through and gave Rosa a fierce pinch; she yelped, and balled her fists to pommel him.

Tears stood in her eyes. Isabella broke away from me and hovered threateningly above Murtha's chair, elbows at her sides and hands open. "Sadismo here not to be permitted," she broke out. "Mi hija esta delicada, don't hurt or nothing, OK?"

Isabella was a very angry naked woman. Murtha looked stunned. "What are we talking about here, a friendly little pinch on the tukus? She really got me, what was I supposed to do?" Murtha turned to me. "You probably don't know tukus."

"I have some idea." That moment I realized that Rosa was not only young; she was *very* young, pretty much a child still. Worse – spotty as my Spanish was – I'd grasped that Rosa was not Isabella's sister. She was her daughter, no more than eleven or twelve.

Where was this taking us? Blitzed as I was, I was still rational. There was no army in Costa Rica, but uniformed police on bicycles were all over the streets.

"Murtha," I said, "I hate to say it but that whisky isn't really agreeing with me. Pain, gas, very bad. I need to walk this off. I'm going to have to leave it to you for a little while to deal with the troops."

Murtha looked up, alarmed.

"Flatulence, it's a family affliction. Maybe we're over-bred or something. I'll pay the rest of the tab on my way out," I said. "I expect you're studsly enough to meet the need around here." Pulling on my clothes I dry-retched, violently, several times. "I'll be all right," I assured everybody, zipping carefully to spare my erection.

"I love you all," I insisted while I closed the door. "A great evening. Overpowering. Memorable."

I paid the tall man and grabbed the first cab outside the door to the Theatro Nacional. I had the worst case of blue balls of my entire life.

CHAPTER V

"So you just went ahead and handed over my last three hundred thousand colones? You are a sport," Sonny said. "With the government's money. I'll leave it to you to fill out my expense account."

"Aren't you the hombre who is always telling dupes like me never to leave any loose ends? That tall guy looked like retired Gestapo. Here." I handed Sonny his condoms. We were walking back from the Teatro Nacional in the dark.

Sonny pocketed the condoms and gripped my shoulder. "You done good. I'm glad I recruited you. You've got the instincts to stay alive at least a week in this business. Unless you run into Murtha again."

"I can handle Murtha. What scared me most was headlines that flashed in front of my eyes: 'Prominent St. Petersburg real estate attorney pulls ten years in Costa Rican slammer for contributing to the delinquency----' Dad wouldn't be particularly understanding about anything like that."

"Probably not." The plaza that fronted the Gran Hotel Costa Rica was coming into view under the klieg lights, the signature statue of some grandee with flaring crocheted cuffs and a sword. "What did the guy say, 'Espionage ain't beanbag?'" Sonny said.

"Politics, not espionage."

The bums were still sacked out around the benches. "It looks to me as if we probably ought to move on this," Sonny decided. He was feeling me out. "If we could arrange to haul our butts up to the Gold Belt tomorrow and track down the pair Murtha was bellyaching about before he shows up we might get somewhere."

"And that would be before or after the fishing?"

"You're like a little kid. Are we there yet? Are we there yet?"

"I'm here on vacation, remember?"

"I'm surprised at you, Michael, I really am. Have you any idea how many gringo lardasses come down here every year, and all they get to think about is the god-damned marlin or whatever? And here you are, presented with the opportunity every pantywaist who ever saw Indiana Jones carve up the tomb robbers yearns for, an authentic action vacation. And all you're worried about is, when does the fishing start? This is disillusioning."

"I'm like that," I had to admit. "I like things predictable. Probably the German-Jewish blood on my grandmother's side."

"I guess so" Sonny said, and sighed, theatrically. "I can dig that. You stay in the hotel a couple of days and I'll be back by the middle of the week. We'll get our fishing in then."

"You're something of a snake," I said. "I never quite realized that, not adequately. How early tomorrow morning are we supposed to start?"

"Early. We eat breakfast separately and you check out maybe fifteen minutes after me. I'll pull the van around into heavy traffic on Central Boulevard over there and you have your stuff waiting and we take off before anybody watching us can pull it together."

"I'm already having trouble keeping my breakfast down," I said. "And I haven't eaten anything yet."

I passed a restless night. Too many hours on airliners followed by that frolic in the Hotel Morocco left me depleted. I all but passed out; around three or four I woke. The little room was sweltering, stuffy. What was probably a gigantic condenser on the flat roof outside my window was chugging for minutes at a time, then sputtering, then back to chugging again. Somebody in the hotel had air conditioning. I got up and attempted to open the side vents of my picture window and stumbled onto the switch for a little ceiling fan, part of the light assembly. I lay on my sheet, empty, completely naked and grateful for what moving air there was, and dropped off until my alarm blatted at five.

By six I was packed and dealing with the desayuno inclusivo in the baronial hall on the second floor. By then I couldn't stop eating – fresh pineapple slices, bananas, casabas, and then a bowl of bran flakes decanted from swiveling globes and huevos revoltos – scrambled eggs with ham bits – and panqueques and some kind of croissant-like rolls that left an oily aftertaste...I didn't care. I was irresponsibly hungry. I never tasted coffee that good. On the music system somewhere a woman's voice was wailing love-songs against a tinkling piano that embellished the salsa beat.

Across the room, near where a waiter in black with a tuxedo bowtie was taking coupons, Sonny sat and watched me gorge myself. As I was going back for my third cup of coffee he caught my eye. His brow went up. I nodded, not that enthusiastically. He checked his watch, then stuffed a 5,000 colones note into a tumbler beside the entrance and left.

I got my bags and paid my bill and headed toward the taxi stand in front. Nobody seemed to want to come after me. The air was noxious with diesel exhaust. A swarm of school-girls in parochial blazers was taking up most of the cobblestone sidewalk. I pushed through and sidestepped a panhandler and climbed into the driver's side of the van. The side-panel was half open.

"Second time around," Sonny said. "I thought we came down here to fish, not eat."

The guidebook my sister Carol had lent me for the plane-ride was badly out of date. She and Buckley had vacationed on the Caribbean coast during their honeymoon. Her travel guide warned that outside San Jose the highways got worse and worse, narrow and impassable and pot-holed. In fact, heading north, for quite a while we found ourselves on a new system of toll roads we might have expected in Northern Europe.

North of the Puntarenas turnoff the landscape got rougher. What had been hills squared off into terraced mango orchards or stands of citrus that ascended into cliffs. The silhouette of jagged peaks edged the narrowing shoulders, signs heralding some distant volcano that overhung Lake Arenal. The roads themselves looked endangered, the treacherous gravel terrain held back by nets of structural steel or boulders piled in rows to restrain the crumbling embankments for miles. What civilization there was looked muscled into place, hard-won.

Shanties tended to crop up wherever there was shoulder enough. Boxes of fruit under rusty corrugated eaves, tethered goats, one sprawl of rotting planks under a sign offering Reparacion de Llantes, repair your tires.

The Class-A road dead-ended at a village called Pozo Azul. We moved directly north on packed gravel, between farms of Brahmin cattle grazing and sheep that looked up and never blinked. Teak alternating with Savannah oak shadowed the road. I was starting to doze off.

Abruptly, feet from our windows, something in the leaves cut loose with a blood-curdling scream.

"What the hell was that?"

"Howler monkeys. If one gets close enough, buzz up your window." Sonny chuckled. "They get the itch sometimes to join the group, and they can get a tad affectionate. They're biters."

"Wonderful."

"Glad to see you've joined us again. Before we pull into Juntas I need to introduce you to your disguise. Kind of like a bathing cap, give you that distinguished senior-citizen look. Bald. With big, white, bushy stick-on eyebrows to match. I thought about including a jowl, but who's going to get that close? We're liable to stumble into your playmate Murtha over the course of the next couple of days, and he can supposedly get hard to manage if he thinks somebody is fucking him over. He is a different animal with his pants on."

"Terrific. I'm very impressed at how thoroughly you've thought all this through."

"There are thinkers. And there are doers. I'm a thinker."

We parked on a side-street and Sonny helped me into my disguise. The bathing cap was very tight and all but cut off circulation across my forehead. Sonny patted into place a kind of quick-drying plasticine filler he squeezed out of a tube before he rolled on a parchment-colored makeup stick to merge my brow-line and around the ears. The eyebrows went on with gum Arabic. He produced a pair of granny glasses.

"The glasses are elective," Sonny said. "Nonprescription. Give you that widely respected faltering-old-college-professor look. You'll need these credentials."

"Perfect. Do I have to carry oxygen?"

"Not a bad idea. Maybe on our next fishing trip. Here." He was handing me a T-shirt with a black bird diving to snap up its prey and the words "*Tear Their Mothering Guts Out, Ravens!*" stenciled on the front. "You're from Baltimore," Sonny said. "Johns Hopkins. Regius Professor Kostas Phrenopoulos."

"But how does this work?"

"It's obvious," Sonny said. "You're an anthropologist and I'm your Native American graduate student. We're a gay couple. "

"I think I'd rather take my chances with Murtha," I said.

Sonny parked the Armada in front of a compound closed in by a wrought-iron fence and overhung by royal palms set out at eight-foot intervals. It was the local town hall and administrative center for the District Abangares. He emerged finally and we circled the block, then wove in and out until he was sure we were not being tailed. "I think we found Murtha's pals," Sonny said. Then, opening out a map on his lap, he gunned the SUV through a series of dusty rising side alleys and pulled up in the parking area of a ramshackle cabin camp that overlooked the clay roofs of municipal Juntas. Cabinas Las Cayuco the sign up top read.

There was a transient bar in front, with home-made tables the tops of which were huge cross-cut slices of mahogany. We parked between planters overgrown with ficus and had a couple of beers, straight from the cooler, with lime. A half-starved hound wandered among the tables. The elderly woman tending the bar got into a high-speed exchange with Sonny I couldn't begin to follow. When that was over she preceded us as we climbed deeper among the cabins until we parked the SUV in front of unit twelve. Across a narrow open parking area was unit fourteen.

"That's their deluxe suite," Sonny told me. "The senora tells me it is deplorable, she is very sorry, but two other Americanos already have the two-bedroom unit rented until the end of the week. They're out now. The senora says they have the habit of going down into Juntas for their almuerzo. We're in number twelve."

We tossed our bags into the unit as the proprietress was leaving. Across the little alley, a peaked-looking Indian chambermaid was stuffing sheets into a plastic bag. "I wish she'd get a move on," Sonny whispered. "I'd like to toss that place a little before they get back." There was a big fixed picture window in front and on the side of our two-bed unit and several on each wall of the deluxe suite. "I think we really caught a break here," Sonny remarked. "I'm going to move the Armada down by the restaurant. They'll notice us soon enough."

Our neighbors made it back shortly after two PM, just as I was drifting off. Their rented Buick sedan kicked up pebbles in the parking area. Our curtain on that side pulled open an inch or so we watched the pair emerge from the car and start around toward the door of their deluxe unit. The man was probably in his early forties, stringy in wash pants and a sleeveless shirt, with a very high – rather academic-looking – hairline. The woman, much shorter and stockier in a pants-suit, marched in ahead of her companion. She looked a little younger – thirties. I caught a glimpse of her face – broad, flaring nostrils, a lot of eye makeup. Her palm came up as she suppressed a belch.

By then I heard Sonny moving something around behind me. He was carrying over one of the night tables, which he positioned halfway along the window. Out of Sonny's equipment rucksack he slid a briefcase and opened out a tripod which supported the knobbed barrel of some kind of audio mechanism. "Behold the Spectra Sneaker," Sonny announced. "Snoops and runs a tape simultaneously. With this monster we could violate a bank vault."

Fortunately, our neighbors had pulled their Buick in deep enough so we had a clear shot at their curtains. Sonny turned a knob: voices.

The woman: "I don't see how you get most of this crap down, Paulie. Me – another dose of gallo pinto and what is left of my colon turns into a hot-air balloon. It could be that's how the Agency expects to get us back. You think?"

The man: "Stay with the vegetables. They're very reliable here. I would bet you anything they serve comes out of the ground the same day."

The woman: "Who'd argue with that? I just wish they'd brush some of the frigging night soil out of the lettuce before it gets to me. Maybe you don't mind. I gotta go get comfortable. Why did I cart so much wool to the tropics? Besides which I think I'm starting to put on weight. My jugunda gadubas are gonna get baked to a golden crisp inside this bra."

The man: "It can get warm."

The woman: "Too personal, right?"

The man: "You have the right to express yourself in your own way, Audrey."

The woman: "God! You are such a live-and-let-live nerd sometimes I don't know whether to applaud or throw up. Here we are, a couple of healthy hairless primates, and I get a cabin-mate whose idea of a gratifying sensual experience is a cold shower."

The man: "I wish the cold water here *were* cold. Or the hot hot. Even the cold is tepid. I would estimate it took me the best part of an hour yesterday to scrub off all that grit, and dirt, and I mean just generally disgusting filth. You weren't there. All those hours in that horrible mine, sloshing along in a foot of slimy water you just *knew* was rife with flesh-eating bacteria? And what have we got? A pocketful of rocks for Langley."

The woman: "So you're saying: This could be a wild goose chase? That would be a laugh. After I just risked my digestion and blew the best part of a week chatting up how many campesinos was that? In every half-baked labor cooperative and two-bit mining collective south of Guanacaste? Passing around all those envelopes everybody bullshitted everybody else were supposedly for 'consulting backup?'"

The man: "I don't think anybody you're going to run into around these parts could give you any *idea* what they've got. Before I got down here I put in at least a month combing out every open source the Agency's got, that's why I caught the assignment.

"Everybody knows there's a little gold. What's got the power hitters Stateside positively *drooling* is all those rumors about palladium. Rhodium. Big strike, major concession. The absolutely choicest scuttlebutt around Langley the week they sent me down is that the minute our beloved Director of Operations puts in for retirement he gets bumped up five minutes later onto the board of Outreach Development. Courtesy of our incomparable Vice President.

"United has a subsidiary, Coyote Creek Resources, and our information is they are carrying on their books options they signed with the previous administration in San Jose to send their technical crews in. Let the big dog eat, unleash the private sector. Except that *now* President Reposa gets herself elected and she is absolutely *infatuated* with the tree-huggers. She's signed one court order after

another to put the kybosh on open-pit development."
The woman: "You think we're stymied?"
The man: "Somebody needs to take it up a level. And I mean by that, somebody well above our pay grade. This operations Houdini who is supposed to land on us tomorrow will probably come up with *some*thing."
The woman: "I'm going to take a bath. Care to scrub my back?"
The man: "It makes more sense for me to take a rest. We ought to keep things uncomplicated. I told you about my wife? By now you must know how much I cherish my yoga and meditation break."

CHAPTER VI

We laid low until the next afternoon, when Stan Murtha showed up in a khaki Land Rover while we were out grabbing lunch at the downtown Bar and Restaurante Los Manges in Los Juntas. The trick for me, Sonny had insisted while we ate, was to keep my distance from Murtha, who no doubt was well trained to penetrate my novelty-shop getup.

"I think this thing is going to fall into our lap," Sonny had decided while we were eating. "Successful tradecraft in the field is mostly a positioning maneuver, and we have hands down got the drop on these bozos. This fried chicken is excellent. Hormone-free. I'd bet you running around clucking in the dooryard an hour ago."

"Mine is OK too," I said. Our table was next to the trunk of a mango tree at least four feet in circumference surrounded by potted ferns. It grew straight up and through the corrugated tin roof. The walls were barred, but windowless. A tall young woman strolled by openly breast-feeding an infant. "There is a feeling about this country," I said. "Close to nature. It infects the politics."

"Finally," Sonny said. "I'm starting to get through."

"You and Dad. This is our home planet too. Still,

maybe all you half-cocked redskins *are* the canaries in the planetary coal mine. She wasn't that explicit, but I had the feeling your kid sister or whatever she is has a thing about Costa Rica. She's where I first picked up the drum-roll."

"Saria? Maybe – I guess that makes sense. She's out there, God knows. Why wouldn't she be leading the parade?"

"She got me thinking. We can't go picking off one fragile democracy after the next in order to scrape out resources to destroy ourselves with."

"Lord love a convert. How about I put you on the mailing list of the Native American Church? Maybe ship you out with the next available spirit quest."

"I'm starting to panic. Does that involve perforations? How can I forget that tribal guy with the ropes through his chest flying around the pole at my wedding?"

"The sun dance? You learn to rise above the pain."

"I'd rather not try. I function at very low spiritual level. I had enough trouble memorizing all that Hebrew for my bar mitzvah."

"We could allow you points for that," Sonny said.

"When does my apprenticeship end? Is this what the fishing is going to be like?"

"Yes, yes, the fishing," Sonny said. "My brother-in-law, the monomaniac."

When we had parked the Armada and walked up, the Range Rover was stationed in front of unit fourteen. I hit the head while Sonny folded open the Spectra Sneaker. Before he had quite finished tuning it I recognized Murtha's voice:

Murtha: "So how many does that make you think we can definitely pencil in for the plus column? Get something happening around here? Go out and demonstrate and shut all these piss-ass little mines down for long enough so maybe those bigshots in the Economics Ministry start missing their kickbacks? *Motivate* these grubby little peons? Condition them to where we tell 'em, gentlemen, shit! By then they're chompin' at the bit to at least throw up."

Audrey: "It's just that these campesinos aren't buying. I've been here laying it out for them all week – look, caballeros, I'm bringing you opportunity. What are you taking home – fifteen dollars, twenty dollars on a good day and your back is broken and you've got nothing left for your wife? You go out and make some noise, strike, get these outdated regulations changed. Help bring modern earthmoving technology to the Gold Belt here. You'll be the foremen, it will be you up there running the draglines. Besides which the company will guarantee to pay anybody with experience a hundred dollars a day, starting. And when I leave they look as if they're buying, especially after I hand each one of them a fifty."

Murtha: "Except that – nothing is happening."

Audrey: "Frustrating. I get the impression we got the most of 'em lined up, and the next time I come around it's 'Alfonso hasn't decided yet,' or 'He says the company has plans to dynamite the hills and bulldoze the jungles flat. We wind up slaves in Gringolandia.'"

Murtha: "Which is how it will probably turn out. And why the hell not?"

Audrey: "The other refrain I hear is, 'Alfonso wants

to wait out President Raposa's last six months.' I got a hunch she tosses the bastard a fish or two to keep everything quiet."

Murtha: "So who is Alfonso exactly?"

Audrey: "He is one obstinate backcountry slob, but he is also the Secretary-General of the Mining Cooperative. They get their unemployment and all that from him."

Murtha: "Obviously, you gotta get to this Alfonso."

Audrey: "I did. We talked. Green, every blubbery inch. He won't even take any consulting money."

Murtha: "So now we know. *He's* your problem."

Paul: "This is a highly traditionalistic society. They can come up with a lot of lip service about their democratic roots."

Murtha: "Is that how it is? Bullshit! I understand these people, I speak the language. I was a rookie around here when Joe Fernandez was station chief and flannel-mouthed old Oliver North was calling the shots against the Sandinistas. We owned *every*body. At least until those chinless wonders in Congress fell apart the day that motherhumpin' cargo plane went down. Democratic roots my ass."

Paul: "So -- how should we approach this thing?"

Murtha: "You gotta get serious. Make an example. When Iran-Contra was cookin' we had a team of fifteen top-level Tico agents we nicknamed Los Babies in there scraping up the dirt on every government official with lead in his pencil. Unfortunately, Oscar Arias got away from us."

Audrey: "But what's next?"

Murtha: "How hard is that? You say this Alfonso Whats-his-face is your problem? Make him your solution."

Audrey: "How can we do that? He won't accept money?"

Murtha: "So we find something he has to accept."

Paul: "I'm not sure I—"

Murtha: "Watch and learn, cowboy."

Paul: "But.... You two work it out. I'm taking my personal time now. Yoga, I'm a yoga adept. Audrey will fill you in."

A moment later there is the sound of a door being pulled closed.

Audrey: "Paulie is basically technical. Not a lot of time in the field. I'm mostly counterproliferation these days, terrorists. Europe and Turkey."

Murtha: "So maybe I don't have to draw you too many pictures."

Audrey: "I got right away where you were headed. You're gonna have to break Paulie in a little easy. He's got these attitudes – I think he's born-again or something like along those lines."

Murtha: "You ask me, that hootnanny is definitely light in the loafers." Murtha spat. "As long as he keeps his mouth shut he won't have problems." Pause. "I bet he's a goddamned barrel of laughs on assignment like this."

Audrey: "He's kind of a sweet guy, just extremely literal. And extremely married, if you get what I mean by that." Pause. "I bet you're probably a wild man. Living legend and all the rest."

Murtha: "I get my rocks off." Pause. "Couple nights ago I was invited to a party in San Jose by this blueblood weenie who's part of the circles I travel in back in Washington. Sisters, advanced as hell. Show up with a dab of KY jelly and maybe a snort of Bolivian Marching Powder and they don't mind takin' it *any*place else the sun don't shine. They got those young muscles, I'm tellin' you. Life on the road."

Audrey: [After an extended pause] "You know, Paulie there is likely to stay in that room for the next hour. I got nothing against that Bolivian Marching Powder."

Murtha: "That's gotta wait. Tonight we're gonna meet your Alfonso What's-his-face. Need to stay sharp. I take it you know where he lives?"

Audrey: "Sure. Yeah. One of those rabbit hutches they live in along the fence that overlooks the river."

Not long before eight we heard them organizing to leave. Sonny and I ducked out and waited in the Armada near the restaurant area. After the Buick went by Sonny delayed until they had made the turn and we started up and began to follow. We were running without even parking lights as the last of the twilight dissipated, guided entirely by the reflection along the gravel banks and off the foliage. When the Buick circled into a shabby residential neighborhood and stopped we eased around a corner and out of sight and climbed out and watched through the lower branches.

A boy of seven or eight went by rolling a hoop and Murtha stopped him and said something and pressed a bill into his hand and sent him down the road toward one of the primitive adobe residences behind the fence. The fence itself was crowned with concertina wire but from our angle the front of the house looked open. A television set was on, next to a small refrigerator and some littered shelves. The boy shouted something and a portly woman in an apron came out, dangling a skillet. She waddled back into the glare bouncing off the television screen and a few seconds later an equally heavy man in a baseball cap unlatched the fence and came out into the road and followed the boy in our direction. He had a face like a frog, open and bulging.

Audrey was waiting in the shadows. The heavy man seemed to recognize her and they got into an exchange we couldn't hear. Audrey stepped back a little and the heavy man pulled a little closer, gesticulating, and I could sense more than I could see a form emerging beside them both out of the shrubbery. "Si, estamos de acuerdo, no?" I heard the heavy man concede; I sensed a sudden powerful movement capped by a profound crunch; the heavy man was sagging backwards, sliding toward the Buick.

Sonny drew me back out of the line of sight. After perhaps a minute the engine of the Buick turned over. "They'll have him propped up in the back seat," Sonny whispered. "No time for the trunk. We don't move until they pull out. As long as we're close enough to see which way they head out of town."

They headed south, then east on highway 131, then a jog onto highway 23 headed into San Jose. There was enough traffic that early in the evening for us to let a couple of cars come in behind the Buick and flick the dims on in the Armada. "Could be they expect to disappear Alfonso," Sonny speculated. "Liquify him in quicklime in somebody's basement in San Jose."

We passed a sign indicating an iguana crossing and

something that called itself a Butterfly Farm, where every light was out. The two intervening cars had turned off and we had dropped back and Sonny was driving by the light of a three-quarter moon. A pair of jet-black longhorn cattle had drifted out onto the highway, impossible to see until we were all but on top of them; Sonny braked with great care, nearly grazed one, but avoided squealing.

The Buick slowed down, eased across a very wide bridge, then stopped.

Sonny turned the dims on and passed the parked Buick and took us around the first bend. "If we stopped, Murtha would know we were onto him," Sonny said. "We'll turn around and head back. See what you can see."

Approaching from the south, our headlights swung through a sign stamped Rio Grande de Tarcoles just before the bridge came back into view. I made out a broad form who was probably Murtha and the lanky Paul, with the bulk of Alfonso slung between them, as if they were assisting a drunk. They were struggling toward the low rail set in hewn stone.

"Very little we can do now," Sonny said. "We're what, an hour and some south of Juntas? Let's go get settled in tonight and come take a look tomorrow morning."

Nothing that had happened so far had left me sickened by the utter ruthlessness of the intelligence community like this. Driving back we didn't talk.

I slept very little that night. I drifted off just before dawn; when I came to Sonny was on his cell phone, working one of his military frequencies. The trio in unit fourteen were apparently sleeping in.

"Big day," Sonny said. "First thing we better go have a look at that bridge over the Tarcoles. Maybe some huevos rancheros to lay a base?"

I couldn't eat much. The bridge had been deserted not long after nine the previous evening, when we had seen it last. We got there around ten in the morning; paddy wagons from the Civil Guard and squad cars from San Jose and Punta Leona were stacked up along the shoulders on both sides of the highway, along with several motorbikes lying on their sides and a produce truck full of cabbages with a high slatted bed and several local taxis. A television crew was filming the workmen in armored coveralls on the mud flats below, several of whom were endeavoring with long poles that ended in wire loops to pull the snouts of three huge native crocodiles away from the corpulent form hung up in weeds and deadheads in the muddy river below.

Sonny had some high-power miniature binoculars. I could make out enough of the face to know it was definitely Alfonso. The crocodiles had torn out his groin and most of his left leg and the adjacent hip. Over the course of the night vultures had hollowed out both eyes and laid open a lot of Alfonso's copious belly. They were still circling, perched here and there on tiny islands of sawgrass and dead limbs. "They like the inner organs," Sonny said. "Livers especially."

Sonny led me around the abutment of the bridge and onto the red clay that descended toward the cyclone fences along the bank that penned in the crocodiles. "Murtha left his mark, if you know where to look," Sonny whispered to me. He indicated the crossed, waffle imprint of Murtha's Doc Marten low-cuts. "He probably went down with a light to make sure Alfonso cleared the lower supports enough so these monsters could get at him. Probably had him out – bad concussion from the blackjack and the rest -- but the important thing was to make it look like everything people found came from the fall, maybe a suicide attempt or something to pin it on. Keep the authorities guessing."

"Disgusting," I said.

"Absolutely. But highly professional."

"Professional. Well, if you say so. Why does it stink so much? I didn't notice it from the road."

"It's an open sewer. Most of the waste from San Jose and the other cities in the Cordillera Central moves through here into the Gulf. Are you offended? Shit is natural too."

"How do we play it next?" Sonny asked once we were headed north again. "Another activity or rest period?"

"You've got something *else* in mind? Jesus, I'm going to call the folks. I'll never survive one more day in Camp Buffalo Hump."

"This you might enjoy. My bosses want me to pick up specimens of the rock this fandango is supposedly about. Find out what ore deposits the corporations are all lathered up about. Special Operations Command has been in touch with one of the local miners who says he'll take us in."

"I've been taken in enough. Take us in where? Those caves that make you wade through some lagoon of flesh-eating bacteria?"

"No. No, no, no. We'll be well-protected. I've arranged for high rubber boots."

What Sonny hadn't mentioned was the ride up into the mountains. Our liaison, Felipe, was about as lean a human being as I have ever run into, a scarecrow in overalls and a blue billed cap with CATERPILLAR stitched around the crown. He drove a vehicle I gathered was popular in the third world, a square-backed four-wheel-drive panel truck with several independent gear ranges called the Hyundai Galloper. Both doors in front were half off their hinges. Felipe's Galloper was probably beige once, but after a decade of tropical sun and impromptu avalanches the color had been bleached and dinged beyond recognition.

Ascending, the narrow roads deteriorated from gravel to sand to what amounted to sharp big chunks of broken granite bulldozed into a back-switching lip little more than a truck-width wide. There were shallow sinkholes every mile as we battered our way up toward the landing which served as the entry to the mines. The system was simple, no doubt dating back to the Spanish colonization. Over many, many generations self-employed miners had chipped their way deeper every decade into the mountain's stone layers. Now there were tunnels, several over a mile.

Sonny filled me in on background. The Reagan years had awakened a flurry of predatory capitalism toward Central America, with pressure from Washington on San Jose to authorize oil drilling and the yawning open-pit gold mines intended to knock flat the hills. Ore coming out of established digs like the Tres Hermanos Mine looked full of promise.

But Costa Rica was white, for the most part, with a well-advertised tradition of democracy, "The Switzerland of Central America." Local environmental groups were fighting back, suing in behalf of the endangered plants and freely roaming wildlife. When earthquakes tore up the railroad beds and the government abandoned railroads, leaving trestles and abutments to rust and crumble back into the recovering jungle, the North-American corporations backed off and let their "exploitation permits" expire. Ore transport could get expensive. By then there were major gold strikes from Peru to Indonesia, with much more corrupt and indulgent governments to negotiate with.

Control of gold mining drifted back to the miners' cooperatives. Each miner was again authorized to dig ore on his own and cart it back to his backyard rastra, a kind of primitive centrifuge that ground up the broken quartz rocks and isolated the gold particles with mercury. This could produce a steady if modest living.

It quickly developed that the effusive Alfonso had been their champion. The midday editions of *A.M. Costa Rica* and *El Periodico* featured above-the-fold long-lens shots of several of the crocodiles and enough of Alfonso to establish his species. He had been identified. He'd picked up flamboyant coverage in *A.M. Costa Rica,* next to the lead on the bestowal of an honorary degree on la Presidenta Reposa in Taiwan.

The extended death notice made Alfonso sound like George Washington out of Mother Theresa, a visionary who lived simply among the people to devote his days to the salvation of the nation's inheritance. Alfonso had told his wife he was going out to meet a friend; sometime after that he appeared to have died unexpectedly, the victim of a bizarre roadside accident. But there would of course be a review of the forensic situation by the Organismo de Investigaciones Judiciales.

"That's exactly what Murtha was after," Sonny

explained to me. "Alfonso gets to be a martyr, but it's nobody's fault. Everybody in their mining cooperative will get the message. From now on they'll take the money and cave when the pressure comes on."

By then we were halfway up some mountain in Felipe's Galloper. The rest of the way got steeper and steeper. At one point we came within an inch of bottoming out; five minutes later we heard an ore truck clattering down towards us as we were bouncing higher into a blind curve and Felipe rammed both transmissions into low and hung his outer tires over the abyss while all three of us squeezed panic-stricken toward the mountain wall and the Galloper slid by the ore truck, lightly scraping the driver's-side door handle, back into shuddering control as three of the tires grabbed.

"You said I'd enjoy this part of our fishing expedition," I breathed to Sonny. I was still stiff with fright.

"Greenhorn nerves," Sonny said. "This guy makes this run day after day." But Sonny looked awfully pale himself.

A couple of the miners, who might have been pure-blooded Mayan, were lounging around the cluttered mouth of the tunnel smoking ganja when we finally made it up to the landing. Both had on sleeveless undershirts and were sitting on overturned plastic pails. Felipe explained that we were experts from an international commission. We needed to check on safety conditions.

The miners obviously didn't care either way, as long

as we didn't interrupt their smoking break. They agreed to let us wear their helmets, which were topped by battery-powered lights. Felipe preferred to wait for us by the entrance and keep an eye on the Galloper. He told us in broken English that he would watch our shoes.

Sonny and I pulled on the rubber boots. The day outside was getting warmer; inside the mine itself it kept getting darker and chillier as we plodded along through cold muddy water, six inches deep most places. Black hoses several inches thick were suspended from the ceiling. "Every once in a while they activate those things and pump some of this water out," Sonny said. The air was dank enough to bite. A heavy mildew stench grew stronger and stronger as we trudged in.

Every once in a while Sonny stooped and dredged the edge of the tunnel bottom with his fingers and pulled up a stone or two, which he kept feeding into his pockets. After perhaps a half hour we rounded one last turn and reached the opening where the mine dead-ended. Power off the generators that ran the pump allowed one light, a single bulb, to dangle from a hose overhead. A litter of rocks the miners had broken out with their cold chisels and five-pound hammers before they took their ganja break had piled up enough to poke above the water.

"Take some of those," Sonny said. "Move around, not all from any one place. Our metallurgists are going to need to find out whether there is anything coming out of these hills except quartz-based deposits. If there is any serious amount of palladium in these rocks all bets are off. Nobody makes ceramic capacitors these days without palladium for electrodes, and it is hard and expensive to find and getting harder. "

"Those guys won't mind if we take samples?"

"I'll take care of them," Sonny said. "They accept colones too."

CHAPTER VII

I spotted the Buick circumnavigating the Juntas town square just as we were pulling in from the north. Sonny gave them five minutes, then took an alternate route back up to the Cabinas Las Cayuco just in case. As usual we parked below and eased into unit twelve once the coast was clear. The hound attempted to follow us. Audrey was standing in the open door of unit fourteen. Sonny took my hand with a cryptic smile and drew me into our unit.

It was a little after three PM. "What next?" I said. "I can live with my overnight change of orientation, but this bald cap itches."

"We'll move on tomorrow," Sonny said. "Isn't this about the time Paul likes to commune with himself? Let's get the Sneaker on the case. My guess is, relationships in there are about to ripen."

I snapped open the laser microphone on its end table. Murtha was holding forth.

Murtha: "So it's your belief he's gonna stand up. I gotta be frank with you. The way he spent the night in the can heavin' his cookies—"

Audrey: "Paulie's going to be OK. You got to understand, operations is new to him. He's here about that palladium. Probably should have left him in the unit last night...."

Murtha: "And who would'a helped? Tuba lard like that fink last night, move that much dead weight around we almost didn't make it. Coulda used a hand truck the way it developed."

Audrey: "We got it done. *You* got it done."

Murtha: "You just got to pay attention. I been a factor around here a good many times since Iran-Contra. Those crocodiles had the making of an asset from way back."

Audrey: "It's just that you knew how. To make that work. Slick."

Murtha: "It's pretty fucking elementary. We feed; they eat. But from here on out this whole operation gets a lot more complicated. The miners go out, and -- what do you know? -- the government cracks down. That we can guarantee: We had the Minister of the Interior on the payroll for years. So now he sends maybe a thousand knuckledusters from the Civil Guard in and gets this disturbance under control. Which drives every airhead over on the left nuts. Now we got mobs in the streets."

Audrey: "So what we're doing here is—"

Murtha: "Hey, you got it, it's all about lightin' the fuse. So then there's riots, and pretty soon the rabble-rousers have got the word and who do they blame but Uncle Sam? They go after American property – Intel has this three-hundred-million-dollar campus in La Ribera. A shitload of semiconductors. Proctor and Gamble, Abbott Labs – a lot of investment. And don't forget all those gated enclaves of American retirees around here. You think our administration is just gonna sit still? With an election comin' up, and all those superPACs lookin' on before they write the checks?"

Audrey: "But how can you be so sure that's all going to fall into place."

Murtha: "Sweet Cheeks, nothin' ever *falls* into place. You *muscle* it into place. Next week a couple of dozen paramilitary neanderthals from Honduras which Joint Task Force Bravo trained for years, that we got seconded to our organization, are gonna get dropped off on the coast under civilian cover. Very hard types, pig-fuckers from the jungle, I know you excuse my French. Very experienced with cocaine and demolition. Get yourself some earplugs."

Audrey: "And you're going to run that too?"

Murtha: "Not me. Maybe you didn't notice, I'm what they call a singleton. They use me to front-run this garbage. I'm like you – they send me in to cut the grass before they drop the bombs."

Audrey: "I *hope* I get like you."

Murtha: "It's one hundred percent experience. No substitute. You showed me a lot of good shit last night. You ever take anybody out like that?"

Audrey: "Never anybody like that. The problem I run into isn't usually elimination, the problem is disposal. One time in Hamburg, for instance, just after 9/11. There were these two ragheads we knew had supplied passports to those Saudis that highjacked the planes. We wanted them gone, obviously, but none of us could get next to either one."

Murtha: "So what did you do?"

Audrey: "Stayed with it. What are the choices? After

almost a month we caught one of the Arabs in a dive on the Reeperbahn. I put the moves on the twitchy little bastard, and in the end I got him back to a room we used. He was pretty high on kif. He wanted action, but I kept stalling his ass, telling him I wouldn't do *anything* without protection. I had a lubricated prophylactic the Agency came up with in Technical Services."

Murtha: "And?"

Audrey: "He actually wanted *me* to pull the damned thing onto that humongous Johnson once he actually got it out, but I wouldn't touch it. In the end he had it rolled down about halfway when it blew his circuits. He started turning black. I heard they used the same jelly those bad boys shot up Marilyn Monroe's bucket. But then we had the problem we always run into around NATO, what to do with the stiff?"

Murtha: "Ain't technology wonderful? So what'd you do, leave it in an alley?"

Audrey: "The neighborhood was too well patrolled, it could have been traced. We had a couple of heavies on payroll trained by the Stasi, and they came by and ground my new admirer up and flushed him down the loo."

Murtha: "The loo? You aren't English, are you? I got a thing about English broads."

Audrey: "I *am* English. On my mother's side. *Now* am I entitled to a hit of that Bolivian Marching Powder?"

Murtha: "Nothin's out of the question, you approach me right. Maybe on your knees?"

Audrey: "I'm expected to grovel? Well – I've been told I grovel like a professional."

Sonny turned the Spectra Sneaker off. "Not much we

can use there. They're getting into war stories. Part of the courtship ritual. When they go out to eat I'll pick the lock and get a few snaps of anything worthwhile lying around. You stand watch – just cough if you hear the Buick.

"The point is, we got pretty much what we came for, and on tape. And those rocks. We'll leave early tomorrow morning. Didn't somebody say something about doing a little fishing?"

We did go fishing. A driver Sonny had retained earlier in the year had a cousin who took people out off the Playa Agulas, a beach near the outlet of the Golfo de Nicoya on the Pacific side. The cousin, Luis, was a short, round, extremely accommodating native with plump cheeks and merry slitted eyes, who wore a billed nylon cap with flaps all the way around. He had a big open plastic skiff and a twenty-five-horse Evintrude, which he kept babying like a first-born. Light squalls came in from time to time, which meant no fishing beyond the reef.

Luis gave each of us a heavy fiberglass rod and a reel he said was set with enough drag to play any of the bigger fish in the Gulf – sea bass, grouper, even tuna. We trolled for a while with big flat pink plastic plugs trailing imitation minnows. Nothing hit. After close to an hour Luis threw out an anchor off a sandbar within sight of the ocean-side developments adjacent to Punta Leona. We would use drop-lines, each with many hooks, baited with chunks of squid and calamari Luis had started pulling from a cooler and chopping up. Mahi-Mahi were down there. Roosterfish, possibly.

There were obviously fish -- something was nibbling

at the hooks, sucking the bait off. I started to jig; something hit my line. It was a red snapper, possibly three pounds, with the tell-tale brown patch of an immature fish behind its bright pink fins. Sonny got a hit and pulled another red snapper in.

Luis was elated: He'd come through. Clouds with the possibility of rain were visible off the ocean side. Suddenly Luis became very voluble. Fishing was a family tradition, he told us. His great grandfather had come over from China as a laborer on the railroads and married his great-grandmother, who came from a family originally from Argentina where everybody went out to sea and hunted whales. It was in his blood. Perhaps a storm was coming. We must pull in the lines and move in a lot closer to shore. High waves could damage the boat.

Sonny and I exchanged glances. "See what you've done," I told him. "Right now I think I am going to go out of my mind. You've turned me into a goddamned adrenalin junkie!"

WAR POWERS

CHAPTER VIII

As November opened the troubles in Costa Rica were breaking out sporadically in the back pages of the American press. Like anything that wasn't condemnatory regarding Chavez and the Castro brothers, dispatches out of Costa Rica now tended to provoke editorial irritability, especially on the right. When two of the labor cooperatives in Guanacaste province picketed the mine entrances to scream about the Luddites who ran Mme. Raposa's Interior Department *The Wall Street Journal* gave the ruckus a column and a half. An indigenous pressure group fed covertly by Wall Street superPacs, *Patria y Opportunidad*, monopolized billboard space to lambaste the regime for kowtowing to Marxist policies. Government regulation would ruin the shoeless majority.

The thrust of conservative editorials as the autumn deepened was that President Consuela Raposa was not really up to governing. One of her sons by her first husband had been arraigned in Paris for smoking dope – the gendarmerie later let him off, but the consensus in the tabloids was that La Presidenta was too feckless to exert control even within her own broken household. One night an explosion blew up the function wing of the Apartamento Montaverde complex, a luxurious assisted-living development in the foothills above San Jose that catered to well-fixed American retirees. An elderly woman in an adjacent apartment, Agnes Sylzk, succumbed to a mild stroke. Her son, a Newark contractor, flew down to institute legal action against both the landlord and the San Jose municipal government. Associated Press coverage highlighted Agnes in her wheelchair, drooling into her pearls.

The apprehension in Washington reached crisis proportions a couple of days before Thanksgiving. Perhaps two dozen men in unmarked fatigues swarmed out of the surrounding jungle and broke into Intel's palatial La Ribera manufacturing and research campus twelve miles west of San Jose, in bucolic Heredia. Hung with assault rifles, the swarthy newcomers herded the several hundred back-office billing trainees along with the horde of technicians trapped piecing together microprocessors into storage rooms and flooded the factory floor with fuel oil. Which they lit. In the resulting sea of snapping flames and the pall of black smoke several dozen workers were burned to death and eight more succumbed to smoke inhalation. Three Americans were killed, two staff and the head of security, a retired Ohio policeman. "Gringo, no mas gringo!" several of the invaders hooted as they scattered through the trees minutes before the Civil Guard rumbled in. Their inflection was hard to identify, survivors insisted, probably some mestizo dialect....

Unmistakably close to panic, Consuela Raposa addressed the nation on television. Several of the

Periodicos had gone public with threats that had just come in to burn down *all* of the Norteamericano facilities that were corrupting the nation, dozens, from Glaxo-Smith-Kline to Procter and Gamble. Wal-Mart must relinquish its stranglehold on the nation's supermercados. The post-Reagan era of economic colonization was over.

On Sunday the Leticia Buchanan show on CBS carried a satellite interview with Consuela Raposa. Her thin voice quavering, her face gaunt and her glittering eyes pouchy beneath her dramatic bouffant coiffure, La Presidenta seemed to be gasping at times as she attempted to frame her responses. Public order was uppermost, that much she stood by and she was prepared to stand by. The guerillas who had now shattered the peace of Costa Rica would have to be hunted down, brought under control, dealt with. It was the government's intention to protect the sacred soil, the irreplaceable environment, of their beloved democracy from every manner of force and intimidation, whether from the left or from the right. If in the end this meant that long-tolerated excesses originating with foreign governments or foreign corporations must be confronted at this moment in the nation's evolution, redressed, the parliament would be expected, naturally, to act.

In this historic emergency she herself had decided that without any regular military, the sovereignty – the integrity – of Costa Rica must be fortified by every available means. The courageous Civil Guard was already stretched much too thin. Accordingly, La Presidenta had requested emergency troops from CELAC, The Community of Latin American and Caribbean States. Bolivia, Uruguay and

Venezuela had already committed forces.

That morning Sonny was waiting around our bungalow in the Pink Streets while Linda got Ten Bears dressed; the two were off to the drag races downtown. I produced Bloody Marys – a Virgin Mary for Sonny. "What do you make of that?" I asked Sonny, nodding toward the screen.

" Right out of the old-boys play-book."

"How's that?

"You are beautiful, but you are slow. Remember when your fellow bottom-feeder Stan Murtha told that woman in the cabin camp they had a slug of paramilitary mercenaries standing by in Honduras – 'pig-fuckers from the jungle?' How could you forget a bell-ringer like that? The idea is, all hell is breaking loose on schedule. The locals can't handle it. Time for Big Brother in Washington to protect every rational property-owner's butt from that hysterical lady president."

"Sounds like she's moving on her own."

"Bringing in real military from those other renegade regimes? You're probably onto something there, I imagine that did come out of left field. I hear a lot of the flunkies around the Director of National Intelligence are starting to get nervous as hell now that the Bolivians expropriated their own electrical grid and Argentina grabbed Repsol from the Spaniards. Democracy is what you want on paper, but whenever the lobbiests get involved watch out. Property trumps democracy. Any day of the week. Remember Allende?"

"And you think something like that is possible here?"

"With a vice president like Alvin Sheel dancing our matinee idol of a Chief Executive in and out of the cloakroom?"

Leticia Buchanan's next guest was Elliott Weinblatt, a think-tank intellectual serving as the Deputy Assistant Secretary of Defense for Latin American Affairs. A small, dumpy neocon from the Bush-era foreign policy wing of the Republican braintrust, Dr. Weinblatt's frozen expression was rendered even harder to interpret by his tangle of pewter-gray eyebrows and his tiny mouth, which barely moved.

"You heard President Raposa," Leticia Buchanan opened. A motherly, constitutionally naive regular on the news side of the network, Leticia Buchanan specialized in soft-balls. "How much help do *you* think the United States is prepared to offer her administration as it slips into crisis?"

"What we are looking at here," Dr. Weinblatt mumbled, "Is not so much a crisis as a conundrum. As in the case of every regional situation we find ourselves forced to confront throughout the Western Hemisphere, in which the components are by their nature asymmetrically organized and subject to the well-known laws of interdiplomatic chaos, no outcome is ever a given. Ever since the eighteen twenties, when President Monroe recognized our overriding responsibility, our need to function as the great power in the region has made it incumbent on us to relieve our less experienced neighbors to the South of lapses of judgment which might in the course of time redound to the disadvantage of all."

"I'm not sure I understand," Leticia Buchanan said.

"It would be counterintuitive, irrational, for us to permit the injection of armed forces from the least stable players in the entire region into a community in which we ourselves are historically so heavily invested, where we have contributed so much."

"But if the Costa Rican government chooses to invite their neighbors in to help them, what can we do, really?"

Dr. Weinblatt's tiny, manicured hands rose, palms out, and pushed off as if to repel the very suggestion. "There are higher obligations," he broke out. "Everybody in the hemisphere is subject to the same historical imperative. The responsibilities of exceptionalism we recognize here in the United States take no holidays. We have no alternative except to control the narrative."

"But how?"

"First, in the traditional manner. Next week we are convening a meeting of the Organization of American States in Montevideo. This array of random collectivists La Presidenta alluded to, CELAC – these people have no legitimacy in international law. At this stage, to impress on Mrs. Raposa how seriously we view this situation, yesterday we mandated an immediate embargo on shipments of vital materials to the Republic – spare parts, foodstuffs, what have you."

"But what if that doesn't work?"

"Then we shall have no choice."

"Send in the Marines?" Leticia Buchanan was struggling to keep her vibrato level. "Invade the oldest democracy in Central America? Didn't I just hear there was a case pending before the Supreme Court about whether the president actually has the *authority* to order that sort of an invasion without an act of Congress. When there is no well-demonstrated national emergency?"

Dr. Weinblatt looked unmoved. "That is correct," he said after a moment. "Technically. We expect the high court to validate the procedures according to which this country has seen fit to defend itself since the second Roosevelt administration. Vermont vs. The Department of Defense in re the War Powers Act is up for review before the Court. We anticipate a workable decision before Christmas."

Later that same afternoon Sonny shoved off for Pease Air Force Base. That final two weeks in November were jammed for me. Word had come down from Washington that I would be expected to appear again before the almighty Supremes the first week of December with back-up arguments relevant to our obscenity – or anti-obscenity – case. The younger clerks relished the screenings, and reportedly had trouble leaving the subject alone. I would be joined by at least one legal gunslinger from The Free Speech Coalition, a lobby underwritten by producers of "adult-oriented material." At issue was the touchy question of the use of *animation* to depict children – or dwarfs, the images themselves tended to become ambiguous – in the throes of accommodating their elders. The lower courts had refused to come up with guidelines. In Ashcroft v. Free Speech Coalition the 9th Circuit had in effect given the film-makers a pass.

Very much a father myself at that stage, I wasn't that persuaded I was on the side of the angels. The precedents were mixed. After a week of tough-minded telephone exchanges, I was resisting misgivings when it came to my hardened California colleagues, their cynicism, their easy-going indulgence of "virtual depiction."

Sonny turned up again a week after we'd taken in La Presidenta Consuela's throaty plea on television. We met at my office to go to lunch. The low-grade civil insurrection in Costa Rica continued to amp up day by day. There had been violent protests and spot picketing at assembly facilities of Motorola and Kimberly Clark. Three Wal-Marts had been taken out during successive nights, evidently by mortar fire. Within SouthCom elements of the reconstituted U.S. Fourth Fleet now lay at anchor off Puerto Limon, several destroyers and a dozen cruisers. Reactionary elements in the National Liberation Party were agitating for impeachment proceedings against President Raposa. Coffee prices tanked.

Sonny was just back, still decompressing. Resignedly, we were grinding through the last months of our military involvement in Afghanistan. Worries around the Pentagon had picked up when it came to the thousands of sophisticated missiles and IEDs and bomb-proof armored personnel carriers that hadn't been accounted for in the final audit but which everybody knew were out there, guaranteed to chew up our troops during the next cycle of violence. Nobody had forgotten the stingers left behind and grabbed by the Mujaheddin after Charlie Wilson's war. Every time a transport took off or landed the senior brass sweated.

Army intelligence had a pretty good idea where most of the arms would probably wind up. They slipped Sonny in to reconnoiter, mark up the hidden depots on targeting maps. Weapons had been spotted in barns and tobacco sheds throughout Helmand Province. The rampaging Gulbuddin Hekmatyar was believed to have restocked storage areas along the Pakistan border and throughout the Northeast. Hours before we withdrew, low-flying sorties and predator drones were scheduled to saturation-bomb the camouflaged munitions and take out anybody still guarding them.

Autherine had just dropped off a compilation of recent first amendment decisions around the district courts when Sonny walked in. He looked – unusual for him – wan, even a little deflated. His eyes looked bloodshot, probably from lack of sleep. My partner and brother-in-law Buckley Glickman ambled by the open door and joined us.

"Back from the empire," Buckley said. "Are we safe yet?"

Sonny sucked in his cheeks and appeared to consider. "Just don't look down."

"Is our esteemed vice president going to get the go-ahead to clean up Costa Rica?" The day before, an aroused Democrat quorum in the Senate had managed to block a resolution that would have permitted the Chief Executive to land troops and restore order. The whole issue was slated to be bucked up to the Supreme Court as a long-overdue test of the War Powers Act, which successive Courts had finessed. Overnight, it had now become too politically risky for the poll-obsessed president to move until the decision was announced.

"Ask your partner here," Sonny said. "He's supposed to keep track of the players."

"I'm just your overworked small-town shyster," I said. "We're always the last to know."

"Could get interesting," Buckley said. "I tell you one thing, those Supreme Court pussies get off their overcompensated butts and let our SEALs break up a little crockery down there and in ten minutes it will be all over but the giggling!"

"It'll be all over," Sonny said, letting his breath out. Buckley was a test.

Sonny and I wound up having lunch in the Northeast Tavern. Tucked away on a side-street, the Tavern had a life-sized manikin in a top hat purporting to represent a boozing tramp hanging out its corner door. The place had the best assortment of beers in Florida, from Yuengling Lager to a couple of rare Oktoberfest Bavarians. Quaffed normally in the twenty-four-hour gloom of the place with exotic sandwiches, Ani Tuna Sashimi and Roasted Portabella a specialty.

"You seem a little preoccupied," I said after a while when our beers came.

"Cultural jet lag. They've assigned me to Afghanistan maybe a dozen times and each time I forget what a downer the place turns into if you're stupid enough to look around. It's like a nightmare that strips the decency out of you after a couple of tours. Two times the commanders sent me around with some recruit from Karzai's patched-together army to show me weapons dumps and each time the kid wound up checking me out until he thought I was asleep before he crawled closer from under his blanket with one of those thick blades they use to butcher their fat-assed sheep. The thing was, I needed the guidance so I pretended I just woke up and never actually noticed. It's just as well my

Pashtun is not the best. On the reservation the 'skins referred to punks like that as 'striplings who shit in your food when you go out of the lodge to make water.' Iktomi, the Lakota elders call this. Spider people."

"Not Westernized, you're saying?"

"Not Easternized. Not anything. They want our money, but after that they want us to leave them alone so they can get back to poppies and feuding and mutilating their infant girls. That nasty little bastard intended to ice me to rack up points with the Taliban."

"And once we're gone?"

"We are gone. We just don't know it yet. We're leaving some very good people spattered across that rockpile. Their spirits can never leave."

The beers came, in big frosted mugs. "You get very tired," Sonny said after a while, "sleeping with one eye open." He hoisted his beer and we touched mugs. "I saw the metallurgists' reports," Sonny said. I must have looked puzzled. "On those rocks. In the mine in Costa Rica."

"What did they tell you?"

"Rhodium. Very rich deposits. Also palladium. The rumors had it right."

"But what's that going to mean?"

"War. Some kind of military action. Like Grenada, maybe, unless there's serious resistance. Then – all out. Somebody has been spending a lot of money whipping all this up, and now they're going to collect on their investment."

CHAPTER IX

I was back in Washington on the Tuesday in mid-November before the Thursday on which we were scheduled to reargue our case. As usual I stayed at the Hilton on Connecticut Avenue. There remains an old-fashioned sweep about the place, a kind of shadowy art-nouveau grandeur that has somehow survived the hotel's radical remodeling. The deferential third-world staff – Ethiopians, Cubans, old-fashioned, deferential blacks – understands how to cater to my need to impersonate a patrician. I am a dedicated breakfast eater, and most mornings the fixed-price breakfast buffet is replete with mangoes and granola.

By prearrangement the pair of lawyers The Free Speech Coalition sent out of California to back me up also arranged to stay at the Hilton. We had the use of a small, second-floor conference room in which to pull our case together. Their position remained that the first amendment meant that there was nothing too raw, too exploitive, to show up in movie houses or rampage around the internet. I argued that community standards would ipso-facto impose themselves and gum up distribution whatever the Court decided, so it was best to agree on realistic guidelines.

While I was around D.C. I gave Saria a call. She said that with Costa Rica in upheaval the War Powers crisis would overhang the docket of the Court until Christmas. Maybe we could get together at least for lunch. An hour later she rang me up to tell me that she had mentioned me to her boss, the honorable Grover Stynehenge, and that the justice was a great reader of Dad's work – especially the Keynes biography – and that Stynehenge had suggested that I join his party for an early supper the next evening, Wednesday, at The Cosmos Club. Off Dupont Circle, Massachusetts Avenue. Six sharp.

I hadn't expected that. Since I would be arguing a case before the justices the next morning, might that not constitute a conflict of interest?

Saria broke off a moment to ask him. "Lefty says to tell you he has no truck with horseshit regulations, period," Saria got back on to say. "He says if you want to buy some influence with him it's going to take a hellova lot more than a god-damned dinner, in particular when he's payin'. Exact quotes, still steaming."

I said I would be more than honored to attend.

As with so many Washington institutions, the membership of The Cosmos Club regards its clubhouse as a Victorian landmark as much as a convenient social watering place. It has a rich agenda of lectures, regular meetings of civic betterment organizations. Four stories beneath a mansard roof, faced entirely with nineteenth-century limestone and horizontal blocks of granite, the Richard Townsend Mansion has made it through renovation after renovation without actually getting altered very much. Which everybody involved intended.

What once was a gently sloping semicircular frontal carriageway onto which Victorian-era ladies could disembark from their landaus under a frosted glass awning during an afternoon rainstorm remains just as serviceable in the age of the automobile. A soft-spoken African doorman in uniform with piping on his sleeves awaits the dignitaries as they arrive by car to turn their keys over to valet parkers. Reputation demands its privileges.

I got there early. Having walked down from the Hilton late on a damp, Mid-Atlantic afternoon, I killed ten minutes on a bench in Dupont Circle while flights of pigeons descended for a communal drink onto the huge basin atop the monument, then rose as a body to throng the surrounding elms. Sparrows hopped around my feet, challenging me with their beaks, agitating for crumbs. But I was uneasy, and I was a few minutes ahead of time when I started out up Massachusetts Avenue toward the Cosmos Club.

I arrived at the club a couple of minutes before six; dark was settling in. Several cars – all dark, all polished and limousine-like – were lined up waiting to be valet-parked. I reached the entrance walking into their headlights. I side-stepped one sedan just being driven off, and through the windshield of the one behind it I caught sight of a generous-bodied blonde woman in a kind of helmet-like, Dutch-girl hairdo easing out from behind the wheel. Next to her, slumped forward, hollow-faced and eyes glittering, an elderly cowman's fringe of uncut white hair splayed out around his collar, was Justice Grover Stynehenge. Saria was in the back.

I had started to step closer when a squat, rather burly man in a soiled trench-coat stepped out from behind one of the enormous globular boxwoods that flanked the entrance and pressed a well-stuffed envelope into the hand of the blonde woman just as she was turning over her car keys to the parking attendant. Caught off guard, she dropped her keys. As she was stooping to pick them up the driver of the car behind her, impatient now, flashed his high beams. I blinked hard, then opened my eyes not three feet from the brush mustache and hectic alcoholic features of Staniford Clinton Murtha, my fellow bottom-feeder – Sonny certainly nailed that.

He recognized me too – something in his face contracted, I sensed that he was holding himself in, upset and fighting the urge to react, violently. I was out of context, a very dangerous place to anybody in the intelligence business.

I thought, frozen – something I should say? But I was blown, Arnold vanden Heuvel was blown. I took a step back, and moments later Murtha had backed into the shadows and lumbered off into the night.

My party awaited me in the vast reception room just inside. It was like stepping back into the time warp. A Frederick Remington-style sculpture of a grazing buffalo. An expanse of embroidered furniture groupings in which the members might take their coffee after a demanding lecture. Veined French marble pillars. Behind a desk near the door a haggard-looking little woman was running up some numbers on a World War II calculating machine.

Justice Stynehenge himself sat restive in a motorized

scooter. Saria introduced us. "Wonderful moment for me," I couldn't help gushing. "I appeared in front of the Court in October. First amendment case--"

"I remember, I remember," Stynehenge cut me off. "Florida, we get a beaucoup allotment of Florida first-amendment cases. Rednecks control the legislature down there, petitions pile up after every recess. Filed mostly by Tea-Party Christians in the boondocks petrified to take a whizz without Jesus steppin' in to hold their consecrated peckers. They expect the Court to protect them from themselves." Justice Stynehenge cackled. "I b'lieve I'd enjoy a drink," he decided. "This my wife Hasna."

We shook hands. Hers was surprisingly moist, and plump. Just beyond the edge of voluptuous, the neckline on her short pink velour dress definitely made the most of that. "We maintain a ranch in Bradenton. Close to where you are. But I like it badder in the District," Hasna said. She had an expansive Slavic face, cheeky, with a pug nose. Her phrases clicked together, animated by the sing-song of the Balkans.

"Her downfall is, she doesn't ride," Justice Stynehenge said. "You know what they say, there is nothin' in this universe better for the inside of a man than the outside of a horse. Goes for the ladies too. Maybe *you* can talk Hasna here into givin' it a try. We have this nifty little ranch down around your parts. You ride?"

"I don't," I said. "My mother rode, for many years." I was teetering. "She had a thoroughbred of her own. Monument."

"Bring her down. Bring her down. You set me in the saddle I am a different hombre. Limbers me right up, on good days I can even bend my fingers to a certain degree."

The maitre 'd drifted in to conduct us to our table. Justice Stynehenge and Hasna buzzed over the Oriental carpet ahead of Saria and me. Saria dropped back. "He's pretty nerved up," Saria half-whispered. "When he got back to their apartment from the court he was all over the lot. Foggy. Then I happened to walk into their bedroom by accident while she was shoving a hypodermic of etanercept in next to his kidney you'd put a pony down with – looked like at least thirty milligrams to me.

"I remember that crud, I used to help the nurse out in the dispensary at Lawton. I found out the other day that Lefty had a bout with TP while he was in law school, and a couple of recurring staph infections not long ago recently. For embrel to work you have to suppress the immune system. Too much can absolutely knock it out. Then Katie bar the door, like the man says...."

"So here Lefty was dangling there in his briefs on the edge of the bed. Legs? -- he looked to me like a last-stage concentration camp survivor. I think a slug of any inflammation blocker that humungous has *got* to leave *anybody* wobbly as a pole-axed yearling. Then when he started to come around a little in the car he started to snap at everybody."

My mouth went dry. "You think she's overdoing the dosage?"

"I think it's getting to his liver."

"You really think she—" Saria didn't say anything. "Pretty unlikely," I said, mostly to myself. But then I thought of Murtha.

By then a couple of busboys were lifting Justice

Stynehenge's scooter over the threshold and into the members' bar. This ground-level bar had more of a contemporary, masculine feel – half-paneled in walnut, above cordovan banquettes perfectly tufted and buttoned. Hasna assisted her husband off his scooter and into a captain's chair.

"They indulge me here," Stynehenge said. "They know I'm not at all fond of that rococo monstrosity of a dining room or the place upstairs, so I am now permitted to chow down near the booze. Also – who wants to get jammed into that tiny, little elevator?" His low-set red-rimmed eyes looked teary. He waved the wine cart away. "I could use a pick-me-up," he confided to the waiter. "Give me a vodka on ice, at least a double, Stolychnaya if you have it tonight. Mention me to the bartender – we're asshole buddies from way back. You new? Haven't seen you around here before."

"I-am-part-time," the waiter said, laboring to bring up the words. He was a tallish fellow in a serving jacket and the mandatory black bowtie, boney, thirties, probably. A cowlick dangled in front of his very high forehead. "I make the-exchange student. From Latvia."

"Great place," Stynehenge said. "Better these days, right? Without the Russkis?"

"Better," the waiter said. "We like it better."

As the waiter retreated Lefty turned to me and winked. "Vodka. You know what he has gotta be thinking. Vodka -- just like Uncle Joe Stalin," Lefty hooted. "How much more evidence does that poor devil need, I ask you? Pinko through and through."

I looked at Saria. If people were worried about Lefty's

liver, a double vodka probably wasn't going to help. Hasna appeared completely impassive, and bestowed a tight little smile on her exuberant husband once his glass arrived and he raised it to her. Moments later her whiskey sour showed up along with our gins and tonics.

While everybody looked over the menus, Lefty slugged off his vodka and quizzed me hard about Dad. He himself had started out on the law faculty at the University of Chicago during Eisenhower's presidency, and palled around with a number of the big-deal economists of the Chicago School. Pretty much a brash Wyoming punk at that stage, shit all over his britches you might say. John Kennedy had appointed him to the Circuit Court after a year at Yale, then Carter bumped him up. He'd read Dad's book about Josef Schumpeter when it first came out. Creative destruction. Works for what's happening here right this minute, what with President Popinjay smiling that tight little go-to-hell smile of his through one catastrophe after another while Alvin Sheel stuffs all his ex-partners' fucking pockets. All this was off the record, of course.

Obviously, I said. I had ordered the Sole Almondine, as did Saria. Lefty decided on the President Taft Crabcakes. It turned out to be Osso Buco Night at the club, and Hasna had that. But now Lefty demanded another vodka.

He drank it much more slowly and reflectively. What were Dad's thoughts about the problem with Costa Rica? Lefty suddenly wanted to know. I sensed the attention of our waiter, walking back and forth with his fingers knitted behind his back once the entrees came.

What my father thought? "I think he thinks we've

seen all this before," I said. "Starting with maybe the Panama Canal." I knew I needed to be careful.

"Starting with the war with Mexico," Stynehenge said. "Although this time might be we're turning the corner. The country got bled white emotionally in Afghanistan, and it just might develop we get to insert enough teeth in the War Powers Resolution so Congress will get off its ass and bite Alvin Sheel's nuts off."

Hasna snorted with laughter; the veal joint she was holding to gnaw on for a moment slipped out and landed in the lap of her dress. The waiter rushed forward to help but Hasna gestured him away.

"That's how we castrated sheep when I was a kid," Lefty blurted out, roaring. "Prairie oysters. Still, Sheel claims to be big on precedent. Think maybe he'd go along?"

"Better not depend on that. You think you have the fire-power?"

"I got my four little collectivist buddies, for sure. After that the Democrats might not buckle once the balloon looks like it might go up. Can you believe it? Could be we're primed to make constitutional history." Stynehenge elevated the dregs of his vodka. "I just wish I felt a wee bit better a lot of the time." He turned to Hasna. "What do you say we hit the head?"

Saria and I watched after Hasna as she marched away beside the justice, slumped in his scooter above his snakeskin cowboy boots. "They'll be a little while," Saria said. "His prostate is shot but he refuses to be catheterized. He lets things get pretty soggy before she changes those dignity britches."

"Why doesn't he resign?"

"Then what? Lefty detests sentiment, but I think he loves the country. In his opinion, he really is enough of a secret Native American to understand how most whites are out to fuck nature up once and for all."

"That's what Sonny thinks."

Saria paused a second or two, then let it out. "Whites are the offspring of Wisa'ka, the great Comanche warrior/god who gives you magical artifacts. Like hydrogen bombs and an economy that melts the icebergs. After you have destroyed everything, our legends tell us we have to stick around as custodians. The red man's burden. Cool, no?"

"Outstanding! Janitors to a Stone Age."

"Lefty still believes maybe he can head it off. Break into the cycle, help reestablish some harmony. Cool down the earth a little, maybe stop some wars. He thinks he's got the swing vote for a reason."

"So where does Hasna fit in?"

"Destiny brought her into the picture to get him through this, Lefty told me once." Saria reached behind herself to position her mounded braids. Her narrow eyes beaded, alert to something moving behind me. Plainly, she wasn't that sure how much I ought to know. "My first few months of my clerkship a Jamaican woman Lefty had had for years came to the office sometimes to administer the shots," she went on. "Then one day last June she called in. I answered. She said she wouldn't be coming around, the service would be sending somebody else. She was sobbing, something was going on."

"And that was?" I shifted in my chair suddenly to follow Saria's glance; the waiter jerked back, his cowlick bounced against his brow. Stiffening, the waiter stepped forward. "I think perhaps a—perhaps some liqueur? While every person waits?" I said I didn't think so. The waiter backed off a step. Saria lowered her voice. "Never found out. A month later he married Hasna. Bang, justice of the peace. His kids from all his other marriages found out when they got the engraved announcements. I watch him working hard as hell scribbling out his endless opinions, he keeps trying, but he is goosey as a virgin in a pickle factory half the time and I absolutely think he's losing ground. She's such a cockwalloper. I think he's afraid of her."

Hasna and Justice Stynehenge were making their way back to the table. "Mission accomplished," Stynehenge assured everybody. He wheeled his scooter around and took his place at the head of the table. "At least a gallon lighter and a whole lot happier." One side of his compressed little mouth went up. "Let's have a look at that formidable dessert cart," he demanded of the waiter. "I know the ladies are up for that."

"Grover tries to make me eat these things so I am strong to look into him. Look after him?" Hasna served herself, a jumbo rectangle of tiramisu. "For every-bawdy." Hasna explained. "In Serbia we share everything. Money when we have some. Food. But not my husband, Grover I keep for me!"

"She is a lot of woman, this lady, but you know what I think? She's worth it." Justice Stynehenge said.

"People ask me, why does a young woman like me marry right now? To stay in America? I tell them: No. I have green card already. Easy for me to become citizen because why Uncle Sam not let me stay? Not enough nurses here anyhow. Eat some!"

The waiter had descended to provide forks. The rest of us each took a tentative mouthful. It certainly was delicious: a foam of ladyfingers in a whipped Italian custard sharpened lightly with coffee and laced with rum. Stynehenge was struggling, his thumb a swollen knot of arthritis and his fingers too shaky to hold a fork. Hasna watched him a moment, her flat nose twitching, then forked up a morsel and fed it to him. Then she reached down and – surveying the rest of us defiantly – scooped up the rest and popped it into her mouth.

"Maybe we order more?" Hasna suggested, and signaled the waiter.

"I'm fine," I said. Saria said that she had had enough.

"What I could use," Stynehenge said, "is one last libation. Vodka, double," he demanded of the hovering waiter. I thought I caught an exchange of glances between the waiter and Hasna. But she stayed quiet, and Stynehenge got his vodka.

CHAPTER X

I got up early the next morning – too early, that gave me several hours to dawdle over breakfast and anguish about whether the additional talking points I had come up with were extraneous, not substantive enough to trigger a useful High Court decision. My hired-gun Free Speech Coalition backup from Los Angeles was mostly apprehensive that the Court would hear me out and consign our case to the "relisted" category, unresolved. After that every politically ambitious county commissioner and every committee of professional virgins in every small town West of the Rockies was likely to demagogue the issue, close down whatever R-rated movies and profanity-laced theater pieces they decided might corrupt the hustings. This ate into distribution.

Independently, my colleagues from LA had decided to submit their own amicus brief -- in case I left anything out. The crux of their argument depended on the Equal Protection clause of the fourteenth amendment – pornographers are people too – supplemented by their insistence that denying an otherwise willing segment of the population access to a film or stage production amounted to de facto censorship, prior restraint, admissible only in national security situations.

I kept quiet, mostly, but I felt they were reaching. If in fact the Court did find for us, the decision would restrict itself to issues a lot more narrow than overarching constitutional considerations. The previous afternoon my colleagues had reserved our little conference room and screened for me a disc of X-rated hits their clients felt deserved open distribution. I had to ask myself how Ten Bears would have felt watching some Eurasian torpedo buggering the bejesus out of an underage Snow White. One of my colleagues remarked that, these days, mixed-race action kept the seats filled. I didn't say anything. I was turning into my father's son.

It was a "sleepy docket" that morning. Ours was the second argument. Number 106 – 1035, Florida vs. The Independent Film Exhibitors Association, got the go-ahead just before eleven. By now the oldest sitting associate, Stynehenge -- already sunken against his high-backed chair in his voluminous black robes -- was seated to the right of the Chief Justice. This was an august presentation: the four pale pillars of Carrara marble, the Burgundy draperies, Old Glory on both flanks....

I attempted to develop my earlier thesis – important art by definition busted the slats out of the categories. Since my earlier appearance before this distinguished panel, *Mit Meiner Scheide Verteidige Ich Das Abendland* had won important honors around the world. Sophie Fekes, the heroine of the film we could all agree gave this epic presentation everything she had, won the Silver Lola, a coveted Deutscher Filmpreis honor. Its director, Karl Schmetterfarb, was selected by a jury in Madrid as the most original filmmaker in Europe. It was runner-up in the respected Hong Kong Film Festival. To deny American audiences this triumph of surrealist cinematography on grounds of prudishness impoverishes our culture. Give it an X-rating, OK. Limit access by age. But please don't cut off our handful of cosmopolitan citizens nationwide from these important cultural accomplishments.

I looked around. In the lawyers' bullpen immediately before the justices, my Los Angeles colleagues seemed to be muttering. Legitimate art films were not what the Free Speech Coalition had sent them East to promote.

I confronted the justices. Three were women, Democratic appointees, battle-hardened bulldogs of the bar.

Community standards evolve, I carried on. While Victoria ruled the waves anything that went on between a woman's clavicle and her knees was out of the discussion, terra incognita. This has changed, utterly. One of the demands of the militant Women's Movement is for a frankness, an equality of the sexes whether it be on the battlefield or trembling heroically in the stirrups. Women's needs, women's expectations, women's demand for total, incontrovertible management of their own bodies. After all, the undraped female form epitomized great Renaissance painting. Women today recognize that: Get it out there, highlight it in best-sellers like *Vaginal Politics*. If women can now unashamedly marry each other, why should the law prevent them from taking in and enjoying such breakthroughs as *Mit Meiner Scheide*?

At this point most of the three deep banks of mahogany pews in the onlookers' area were filled. I stopped to catch my breath; something between a sigh and a groan of approval rose from the heavily female ranks of onlookers. But they weren't all ladies. In the middle section, in the second row, I found myself staring straight back into the wet, discrediting stare of Stanton Clinton Murtha.

I looked away and attempted to brace myself. It was now time for questioning from the justices. Predictably, the first volley came from Associate Justice Victor Scaliponi, a Reagan-administration appointee, point man for the Hard Right. Pudgy, elliptical, Scaliponi, had a reputation for putting the one question that blew up the exchange.

"Attorney Landau," Justice Scaliponi opened, "You are to be congratulated on your industry. Your eloquence. Your attempt at historicity, a rare commodity around this courtroom *these* days. My only hesitation – I admit, a niggling one – goes to the *veracity* of your argument. Have you by any chance perused recent studies on the subject? Ten percent of all adults admit to a measure of addiction to internet pornography, with seventy percent of younger men visiting a pornographic site a minimum of once a month. A majority of our pastors call this development their most socially damaging issue. Relationships are dehumanized. Couples collapse into divorce."

"But I have not been lobbying for pornography."

"I assume you've taken the time to peruse the amicus curiae brief submitted by your colleagues from California?

I had a look at several of the features they would like to see in wider distribution. Gross, really – a smut-hound's banquet!"

"These attorneys have joined the Florida Exhibitors in the effort to help encourage the courts to provide us a more meaningful definition as to what is permitted," I said.

"So *that's* it!" Judge Scaliponi was playing to the gallery – a smug smile, washing his chubby fingers together in the air. "I think we find ourselves a long, *long* way from the guidelines in Pope Paul VI's 1968 encyclical. They tell me Nunsploitation is very popular in France right now. Must we countenance *that* next?"

Justice Stynehenge's eyes opened. Unexpectedly, he broke in. "Victor, why do I think you got a tendency to give Attorney Landau here way too much credit? Dollars to donuts he hasn't come close to molesting a nun for quite some time. Probably an excellent family man. You got a family, Attorney Landau?"

"I do," I said.

"And you wouldn't want them exposed to phantasmagorical sexual goings-on? Crank up any unappeasable appetites?"

"I wouldn't," I said. "Definitely, I would not."

"So let's step back," Lefty Stynehenge said. "Return to earth."

Laughter in the court was general.

Victor Scaliponi hunched forward, both hands clutching upwards. "Sex is reserved for two things. Babies, and marital bonding. Beyond that is desolation of the spirit."

Justice Natalie Roth, a late Clinton appointee,

spoke up. Wizened, with a humped nose and a frizz of unkempt gray hair, emotion had started to hollow her soft voice into a near croak. "Why do I think Justice Scaliponi and I must be looking at different studies? The ones I've run across would suggest that sexual urges are part of our physiology. By way of a glandular requirement, as inescapable and recurrent as peristalsis or the elimination function? Except for our traditional concern for the susceptibilities of children, what business has the court in any of this? Should we mandate bathroom habits?"

The exchange went on, less heated with other follow-up questions, until my question period was expended. A break was scheduled before the next oral argument. I left through a horde of unruly teenagers being herded into the courtroom by their civics teacher. I was barely out into the cavernous Great Hall when I felt somebody tapping me on the shoulder. Murtha! – I froze. But it was the Clerk of Court, to advise me that Justice Stynehenge had requested that I be conducted briefly to the justice's chambers.

Seniority assured Stynehenge of a posh, commodious retreat. With separate offices for a secretary and Saria, Stynehenge's study looked more like the library in a Georgian mansion than unused storage space in which to shuffle through his paperwork. High-posted, with one wall given over to what must have approached several hundred volumes of the Court's official history, The United States Reports, almost everything else reflected Stynehenge's go-to-hell Western origins.

A statue of a pony express rider strained forward on his pinto pony to deliver the post. Navaho rugs were pinned up above the moldings. A stag head between the high windows with one of Stynehenge's ten-gallon hats dangling from its antlers.

Above the walnut desk was a large painting of a bleached cow's skull against the receding desert. "Get's to you, am I wrong?" the justice chortled, having caught me looking at the painting. "Georgia O'Keefe. On loan from The National Gallery. Worth more than I am, any day."

He had parked the scooter next to his desk and was bumping along between two canes, returning from his lavatory. Things obviously hadn't gone that well: he smelled of cigarettes and more: like an unchanged baby. "My rig there gets me around pretty good," he said, somehow reading my thoughts. "Except that half the time I feel like a two-year-old."

"You definitely get around," I said.

"Well – I got a lot to do. We're jammed up worse this term than I ever saw it." He had settled in behind the desk. "You added a lot to dinner last night. Plus, I specifically wanted to assure you you made your points this morning. Might just be able to ease off some on the obscenity guidelines once we get around to drafting the majority opinion. We'll have to see what we can accomplish in the conference." Stynehenge rubbed his eyes. "You leave it up to Vic Scaliponi and his crowd, you'd have every fun-loving secretary in America rattling around in the stocks. Those bozos are *terrified* of poontang."

"Social questions are hard."

"Social questions are treacherous. National security questions are hard."

"You're talking about Costa Rica."

"What else is there to talk about?" Stynehenge plucked on his nose. "That whole thing stinks, I remember when some of those slimy goddamned operators around Reagan were pushing to get us into a war with Nicaragua. Iran-Contra. Same propaganda barrage, a lot of time and money hobgoblinizing the living shit out of the Ortega brothers. Inflammatory incidents. Just lucky Ted Kennedy and Eddie Boland got in the way in time."

"You think this is like that? Some kind of set-up?"

"Smells the same. Orchestrated, with Murdoch and all those other deep thinkers pounding the drum like madmen. The question is going to be: Will the Democratic Congress buy in without a declaration of war?"

"The War Powers Act?"

"Right. Definitely. That case is scheduled to come up just before Christmas. The Almighty and Hasna permitting, we might just compel those pipsqueak politicians to take the whole deal seriously."

This was my opening. Was I getting some kind of signal? Should I mention Hasna, and Murtha, and injections?

"Mike," Justice Stynehenge said, "I thank whatever gods may be for my absolute peach of a new wife. I get my strength from her, that is a fact. What time you got?"

Justice Stynehenge had less than ten minutes to return to the courtroom.

"Never even offered you a drink," the justice said. "We'll make it two the next time. You tell that father of yours *I* think he's overdue for the Nobel Prize."

A bailiff had appeared to assist Stynehenge with his

return to court. Just as he hobbled into the hall I spotted Saria standing in the doorway of her little office in a fringed dress. Her black, glossy hair was down.

"Different presentation, right?" she demanded. "Like the before picture of a squaw on a weight loss program."

"You're not fat," I said.

"Full bodied, is how you'd put it?"

"I wouldn't put it."

"So – is Hasna fat?"

"Hasna is built up. Nobody to tangle with."

"You've got the moves, I'll say that for you. How'd your argument go? I couldn't make it."

"We got a little far afield. I thought I was in there to explain the computerization of eroticism, and Justice Scaliponi started climbing all over me about the decline of the West."

"I always thought you were. Responsible."

"Me as me? Or me as white?"

"Everything. What did you think last night?" Saria frowned. "Is Hasna polishing him off?"

"Lefty obviously doesn't think so. He's still very shrewd. Fragrant, at times. But shrewd."

"I'm glad you noticed that. The shrewd part. Broken down as he is, underneath he thinks he's still Mr. Machismo. Except his body has messed with him a little." Saria touched my shoulder. "He's taken a shine to you, lad."

"I'm just passing through. He's got some real assets. He's got you."

"For what little I can accomplish while she's in the

picture. Hasna." Saria rolled her eyes. "Talk about a snow job."

"She's convinced him she's his lifeline," I said. "What choice does he have?"

I got a long look. "You know, I think my sister's actually lucky. If circumstances were different, you might be worth a good woman's attentions. Bedlam underneath the buffalo robe? Awesome! With you there's more going on than meets the eye."

"Thanks. You're not as full-figured as people say, actually."

"What a pill," Saria said. "I've got to get back to work."

I ran into my gunslingers from the Free Speech Coalition in front of the huge, presiding statue of John Marshall on the ground floor, headed for the airport. I didn't mention Stynehenge, but I did say I thought we stood a pretty good chance of working toward some marginal relief. Both had obviously concluded that I had missed my once-in-a-generation chance to set off major legal fireworks and force the first-amendment issue once and for all. That I had turned out something of a wuss, another small-town lawyer with an overloaded briefcase.

CHAPTER XI

Upon noticing my clip-on authorization pass, a guard consented to let me out one of the side doors into an empty courtyard around a fountain putting up a constant, solitary plume of water. But the exit there too fed back into the front, onto the long, long sweep of steps below the eight monumental columns. Murtha would be waiting; I had *no idea* how I could handle that. It looked as if half the teenagers in the country intended to swarm in to hear the next case argued, shouting back and forth through the chilly fog, caught up in fond, ferocious interludes of grab-ass, wriggling away from the frantic Capitol cops circling to prod them into line.

In San Jose Sonny had emphasized that it was important to keep anybody watching you from finding out where you were staying. Best to take the Metro. I headed up First Street, which seemed surprisingly empty, then west on Constitution for a block or two, then angled back on Delaware into Union Station Plaza. Nobody behind me that I could tell. The Plaza was always crowded, ideal for losing somebody. In one of the arcades I ducked into a shop of embroidered caps and tie-dyed T-shirts and eased out the back and followed the noon surge scrambling toward the Red Line.

I fed several bills into the system and let the turnstile eat my ticket and jumped aboard the car headed in the Shady Grove direction just as the doors were closing. Not followed. There was a seat, but I was up and lost in the melee exiting at Gallery Place before bolting down the iron staircase to the next level, plunging into the mob, then up again and onto the Red Line platform just as the next car pulled in for a couple of minutes hurdling toward Metro Center. Within seconds after we jerked to a stop the car had emptied itself and a mob poured in and caught me standing with one hand gripping a pole, staggering for balance against the crush of commuters. I clutched my bulging briefcase with all I had, white-knuckled.

"*Next station, Farragut North*," a mechanical voice crackled. Everything slowed down for what seemed barely a minute but before I could slide into a seat a heavy new influx of shoppers and noonday vagrants and jostling business types was squeezing me back against my pole. There was a very fat man in a sleeveless undershirt and tattoos, whom I could smell, and, muscling backwards against my thighs, the rump of an Asian schoolgirl with plump cheeks and a jewel-encrusted ring through one of the nares of her widespread tallowy nose. Against my will, my equipment was already responding. She swiveled her face around and inspected mine: eyes like hazel marbles, beneath amazingly extruded lids.

I attempted to slide a little sideways, gasping in the musty air, and I was belly to belly with Murtha.

He looked me over for a moment with that desolate,

seen-it-all expression of his. His pursy little eyes were pebbled, I realized up close, a disgusting pink all the way around. Still a little out of breath, open-mouthed, he patted himself to smooth the unkempt lozenges of his pale regimental mustache while exuding a sour after-aroma of rye. "I had you pegged as squirrely as a bastard," Murtha huffed. "Now it turns out you're a goddamned crowd-fondler."

"What's this all about?" I said. "What're you after?"

"I liked that move you made at Gallery Place," Murtha said. "Out when the train stopped and down to fake it on the Green Line platform and up again in time to jump on the next car. Amateur night, but what the hell? You can take that fucker to the bank, what we gonna call that from now on, the vanden Heuvel maneuver? Pick that cocksucker up in escape and evasion drill? Maybe at the Farm?"

"Maybe I'm just—"

Murtha cut me off. "You conned the shit out of me in that Costa Rican cathouse," he admitted. "I got to give you that. Couple of asshole buddies out for a good time? Made sense to me. Even when I seen your face outside that club last night I figured, hey, that could happen. Sumbitch travels in big-league circles, why wouldn't he pal around with a justice or two? But then I drop by the court to check things out and who's that up there honkin' away in the lawyers' paddock—"

"The lectern, they call that," I said.

"You bet your ass they do," Murtha said. He was too talkative, too tense – I felt him working himself up to something—

"Some kind of coincidence? Only then in my gut I start to realize I was gettin' played for a sap. I don't like gettin' played for a sap. Because sitting there I got the picture, in spades. We're workin' competing contracts. Except you obviously got the inside track, what with the fact that you're a lawyer and all. Attorney Landau, who's gonna beat that? You get to work this thing from the inside."

I was beginning to quake. "Murtha," I attempted, "Whatever you're talking about, you are way off base. To start with, I have never been to Costa Rica...."

"Yeah? So tell me, how do you know my name?"

I had to swallow hard. "A lucky guess?"

"That was inspired. Go tell the Agency you need the refresher course."

"What do I have to say?" I blundered on. "You've got the picture all wrong."

"So you tell me. Lemme tell *you* something. Everybody's got his prejudices. Some people don't like cats. I don't like coincidences. You let the motherfuckers run their course, they pop up when nobody is expecting it and break your ass. Who wants that?"

Next station, Dupont Circle, the mechanical voice announced. The schoolgirl from Asia found a seat. I had definitely lost interest.

"The way you cope with coincidences is to make sure they can't happen again," Murtha concluded, his voice husky. The train had started to slow down; it shuddered lightly to a halt. "You're not that bad an actor, don't hold me personally responsible," Murtha said, his chin brushing mine. "Ima stick you like a hog." The stench of rye was overpowering. Just then the doors had started to open; another horde was pouring in. Murtha lifted one stocky leg and his cuff got pulled up and I glimpsed suddenly a sheath strapped against his calf and the hilt of a long knife.

I resisted stammering. "All right," I said, "Let's say you've got it figured. We're working the same operation. My employers are starting to have doubts, they're not that sure anybody can trust Hasna. I've been brought in to make sure what needs to happen happens. On schedule. They think you're out there running up the expense account, and--"

"It's *happening* on schedule!" Murtha erupted. "What in the fuck makes you think—"

"At senior operational levels people aren't that sure." I was winging it, grasping at straws.

"What senior operational levels?" Murtha's face was purple. "Who is it you think you're workin' for? It's time you got your shit together, you Ivy-League stool sample. Dream on, I got impunity, I get my instructions directly from Sheel's top honcho. That's where it all stops, *nobody* trumps the Vice President of the United States. So you can stop bullshitting me now, Arnie, you don't know what the fuck you're talking about."

Murtha kept his face up against mine, but one of his hands was making its way toward the knife; he obviously intended to deal with me just as the incoming mob was jamming into every inch of space and leave me standing there, packed in spilling out my guts, while he worked free and out onto the platform and up.

I couldn't think; thank God I didn't have to. One of his Doc Marten lowcuts edged forward as he was withdrawing the blade and before I could decide anything I stomped down with everything I had on the tip of his boot. A kind of suppressed bellow came out of Murtha; I felt my heel crushing a couple of his toes. Both his hands came up to grapple me but I had already lurched backwards, scrambled out onto the platform and toward the illumination at one end while behind me Murtha stumbled, dragging one leg, in urgent pursuit.

I reached the narrow escalator packed with every kind of transient ascending slowly to earth level no more than a hundred feet ahead of Murtha. Above – far above – the endless black tunnel of cast concrete up which we were riding burst into daylight, like heaven in one of the Dore engravings from Dante's Inferno in Mother's dressing alcove. I pushed with what I had, briefcase banging against my knees as I elbowed brusquely by shoppers glad to rest their feet and mothers with infants and sagging working people going off shift. Murtha was shoving along too, but I was gaining.

I made it to the misty square itself well ahead of Murtha. Behind three street musicians, one with a tuba, the other two fiddlers sawing away in hopes of more bills stuffed into a dented cup, a line of cabs was waiting. My hotel was just up Connecticut Avenue, but Murtha had better not figure that out too soon. Waiting for him to surface, I found myself reading the quotation carved into the gigantic curve of granite facing above the escalator. "THUS IN SILENCE, IN DREAMS, PROJECTION, RETURNING, RESUMING, I THREAD MY WAY THROUGH THE HOSPITALS: THE HURT AND THE WOUNDED I PACIFY WITH SOOTHING HAND. I SIT

BY THE RESTLESS ALL THE DARK NIGHT – SOME ARE SO YOUNG; SOME SUFFER SO MUCH – I RECALL THE EXPERIENCE SWEET AND SAD,..." WALT WHITMAN, 1865."

Somehow that quieted me down. A society that would preserve an emotion this delicate for a century and a half is probably worth protecting. By then I saw Murtha's head and heavy shoulders bobbing into view in time to spot me climbing into the front cab. I told the cabbie to take the first left and keep circling. Once I was satisfied that I had shaken Murtha I let the cabbie drop me off at the Hilton and wait until I came out with my bag so he could run me over to Reagan International. Whatever would happen next, I wanted it on home ground.

I caught an afternoon non-stop that got me to Tampa in time for Linda to pick me up before her early-evening assistant manager's shift started at Walmart. I had been after her to give up working, but years of money worries after her first husband Savage Owl jumped ship had left her craving a job of her own. The big news that week was that since Sonny was catching most of his assignments out of MacDill, he would be picking up credits toward his PhD in Environmental Sciences at the University of Southern Florida. He'd be around more.

I'd reached Dad just before I boarded the airliner from Washington. Murtha – the people behind Murtha – probably weren't done with me yet. I didn't want Dad to find himself blind-sided. He had a late seminar, but promised to stop by at the Vinoy for a drink at seven.

CHAPTER XII

We arrived at The Pink Streets and turned off Serpentine Drive just in time to intercept Sonny and Ten Bears and Penelope piling into Sonny's khaki Chevrolet Equinox in front of our bungalow off the Oval Crescent. They were headed to Lake Vista Park, blocks away, so Penelope and Ten Bears could race around together in the penned-in dog compound and get their backed-up energy – and, in Penelope's case, a good deal more – out of their systems.

It requires the droll and very often perverse mentality of the Florida civic planner to call Lake Coronado a lake at all. It is a mud-hole, its shoreline latticed out with interwoven weeds, half a swamp. There is a sign stuck into the ooze adjacent to the running track that skirts it on the north reading *Do Not Feed OrMolest Alligator*. Very few are tempted. The presiding alligator is rarely if ever seen, although his cousins and his uncles show up in swimming pools all over the neighborhood. Birds – storks, big terns with crooked beaks, ducks, pairs of snowy egrets, on occasion a dignified blue heron or a fluffy pink spoonbill, the unexpected vagrant pelican flapping over from one of the nearby docks – at one time or another most of the bird population around Southern Florida seems to descend on Lake Coronado, their designated slum.

The immediate neighborhood is black, mostly, but self-respecting black. People nod on the foot-paths. Squirrels stand their ground or run over your feet. There is a recreation center and tennis courts that bake, empty, all through the sultry heat that ends with the hurricane season.

Ten Bears had remembered to bring her well-chewed rubber hambone for Penelope to fetch. At four-plus his sinewy little frame and watchful manner were a constant pleasure to Linda and me. Ten Bears had her hair, ink-black and wiry, which she herself shaped and scissor-cut into a kind of Amazon-basin Prince Valiant that classmates in nursery school teased him about. Ten Bears brushed that off.

Inside the dog compound Penelope knew exactly what to do. She sat and lifted that snubbed muzzle and waited until Ten Bears was twenty-five or thirty feet out under the ragged pines and live oaks and ready to side-arm the hambone for Penelope to snag once it started coming down. Her timing was perfect, over and over again. The moment the ham-bone had reached the top of its arc Penelope cocked her back legs and prepared to spring. Each time she picked it out of the air five or six feet off the packed earth and trotted back to Ten Bears to receive a rough congratulatory mauling, several seconds behind each ear.

Sonny and I settled onto a bench to watch. He seemed less overhung by his Afghanistan mission; the whites of his eyes had cleared up. "How is your case going?" Sonny wanted to know. "Have you made the world safe for pornography yet?"

"You and Dad," I said. "It still seems worthwhile to me. Why let the blue-noses take the fizz out of our collapsing civilization?"

"I guess," Sonny said. "So everything went off as planned?"

"Pretty much. A couple of incidents, though. I kept bumping into Murtha all over town. Thanks for introducing us. He attempted to disembowel me in the subway around noon today but I ran for my cowardly little life. Otherwise—non-eventful."

"You are more trouble," Sonny said, "than all my wampum. You better take it from the top."

I went over everything. "You by God definitely have mastered the agent handler's knack for being in the wrong place at the wrong time," Sonny observed. "Murtha talked too much. He probably knows that."

Sonny sucked his cheeks in, and pushed out his slit of a mouth. "Based on your gut-wrenching little tale we are dealing here with chicanery on the grand scale, like, say, Watergate. This isn't some brainstorm a mid-level knuckle-dragger in a basement office at Langley came up with between coffee breaks."

"Is that good or bad?"

"Probably good, on balance. If Vice President Alvin Sheel is really pushing to subvert Costa Rica and grab off the mineral deposits, he is probably savvy enough to fold his hand before the roof falls in. Bush Senior was the guy in the shadows in the mid-eighties when the Contras were flying guns into Honduras in U.S. military aircraft and hauling cocaine back in the same transports to Opa Locka. Then all that got too problematic. Even Oliver North decided we could live with the Ortega brothers. Politicians blow hot and cold, even greed-heads like Sheel."

"But how do you do that?" I wanted to know. "Run the newsreel backwards? Get them to back off."

"A lot of the time sunlight works. Always the best disinfectant. Feed information enough to the right Congressman. Find the right newspaper guy, if there are any still employed."

"Dad has some contacts," I said.

"This can take finesse," Sonny said. "The Agency was evidently brought in early, and by now several of its subversive warfare supremos are liable to be implicated. All those bombings, the propaganda and the rest of that – that requires a fair amount of logistics. And budgeting, and people on the ground. A professional heavy like Murtha was laid on during the exploratory stages. From outside, a contractor. Willing to do anything, easy enough to disavow, known to be experienced with wet work in case it came to anything like that."

"But where does the vice president fit in?"

"Sheel is notoriously activistic. Doesn't trust the bureaucracy, a Bobby Kennedy type. Wants his own guys involved, people he controls directly. Like Nixon and The Plumbers -- high risk, high reward. Apparently Sheel grabbed up Murtha, but now you've obviously got Murtha spooked that you might displace *him* the way he took over from those stiffs in the Agency."

"His pride is hurt?"

"His pocketbook is hurt, potentially. I'm sure

Sheel's backers in the mining cartel have got no problem parting company with a couple of million dollars Canadian to make sure Stynehenge isn't still on the tracks when the time comes to railroad through the resolution to invade. Murtha was probably booking his retirement villa in the Cayman Islands, and here you come along and maybe he's out of the picture."

"You had to be there," I said. An Airedale and some kind of yippy little terrier had noticed Ten Bears and Penelope and were racing over to intercept the hambone; Penelope stood her ground and emitted a low, throbbing growl that backed them off.

"Don't apologize." Sonny gripped my shoulder. "You are still alive, you're already beating the odds every minute. Didn't I tell you you have talent?"

"Sonny, look – what am I supposed to do?"

"The trick is, not to take everybody on. At least, at once. Besides which—" Sonny looked thoughtful.

"Besides which what?"

Sonny obviously thought of something, then held it back. "You're starting to develop into a halfway decent attorney," he managed, finally. "It might be practical to keep you alive."

Just after 6:30 we headed for the Vinoy. Capping Beach Drive and overlooking the yacht basin, the Renaissance Vinoy St. Petersburg Resort and Golf Club has been up for renovation towards the end of every recession, with costs unavoidably running into the tens of millions. Its posh, darkened lobby of random glazed tile and antique Oriental carpets runs on for block after block before opening into the gleaming dining room. Halfway along is a discreet bar. Most visitors prefer to retire to tables on the porch beyond the huge arched windows, sipping their frosted highballs and watching the sailboats across the avenue tacking in and out to make their slips.

Dad wanted to talk, and was waiting for us inside, where there were sofa groupings and we wouldn't risk running into anybody. "Ahoy, Sylvan! Welcome to the yacht club," Dad greeted our son, standing. Ten Bears looked a little startled. His Indian name had caught on in pre-school and he had half forgotten that he was also named after his grandfather. With characteristic aplomb, Ten Bears recovered and raised a fist to bang knuckles with my father.

Technically, children weren't encouraged to sit in where alcohol was served. But the evening manager was an acquaintance of Dad's. He swooped down and proposed a Promenade Punch for Ten Bears, only with no rum. Sonny asked for that too; Dad and I were up for Hemingway Daiquiris.

I suppose I wanted to hear what Dad thought. But should I load him up with worries about me? Besides which, how could I not feel chagrin? My problems were my problems. It might be smartest to stick to the trial.

"I think I made my case," I said before Dad could ask. "Right afterwards Justice Stynehenge summoned me to his chambers and told me I did all right."

"*Lefty* Stynehenge?" Dad perked right up. "Now there's a blast from the past. Gave all those shvitsers around Reagan fits, even George Shultz, who I always thought made some sense. Stynehenge -- kind of a late-blooming New Dealer, rode in on his horse and trampled everybody's grapes of wrath. Didn't he come up when we were talking with Sonny's sister?"

"Good call," I said. "Justice Stynehenge is very high on you. Reads all your books. Starting with that treatise on Schumpeter."

"Treatise is right. Michael, I doubt that *I'd* be able to read the damned thing today, except maybe at gunpoint. How's he doing?"

"Not that well, actually. Pretty much a basket case from rheumatoid arthritis."

"That's bad news," Dad said. "They're going to need him front and center the day that war resolution thing hits."

"He expects to be," I said. "If he makes it."

"*If* he makes it? Jesus, I sincerely hope he's going to make it. One more Supreme Court appointment by that space cadet in the White House and--" But Dad gave it up. He was looking at me, eyes goggling out a little, moistening his upper lip. Our punches and the Hemingway Daiquiris arrived. Ten Bears slid out his a straw.

"There are complications," I said. I was hesitating; probably I had already gone too far. "Lefty isn't doing well," I said, "and there is reason to believe he's getting a little help with that."

"Help with what? Help with dying?"

"It happens that a guy Sonny and I ran into in Costa Rica turned up in D. C. Kind of a covert specialist. Sonny's sister Saria thinks he might be mixed up in a kind of conspiracy to get rid of Stynehenge."

"Now I *do* need a drink," Dad said. He took a long sip of his Daiquiri. "I think a little too much sea salt around the edge. At these prices, they probably don't want to scrimp." Dad's voice dropped. "How involved are you in this?"

"Involved? In over my head was maybe a month ago."

Nobody would say anything. Ten Bears slipped off of the couch and took a position closer to the bar so he could very somberly examine the sallow Latino in what looked like black pajamas and a pony-tail who had started to strum absent-mindedly on an electric guitar, one leg cocked out. After perhaps a minute Ten Bears skipped toward us and slid back into his place and concentrated on bubbling up the pulpy residue in the bottom of his Promenade Punch with his flexible straw.

Dad was still looking at me. Wearily, I provided some details.

Dad turned to Sonny. "Isn't this your line of work? What should Michael here expect if this plays through at all?"

"Depends on Murtha," Sonny told Dad. "Mostly on whether Murtha thinks Michael is competition or possibly some kind of whistle-blower. Then he would want Michael out of the game, right away."

Dad looked at me, and let his mouth fall open, and rolled his eyes. "Red man speaks truth," he decided, straining to keep it light but looking very grave. Dad shrugged and addressed Sonny. "So tell me something. What do you suggest?"

Sonny hesitated. "Play keep-away," he proposed

quietly after a moment.

"How is that played?"

"This thing is bound to be over by the end of the year. This town is your turf. If Mike never really shows up Murtha won't have a target in time. After that it'll be too late."

"Wonderful," I said. "Except that I have a family to raise. A law practice. Penelope is a lot of responsibility."

"Fake a trip. A leave of absence. Work out some way to mail it in until Costa Rica is up or down."

"But doesn't that make me a coward?" Neither of them said anything. "I like Plan B a lot better," I said. Except that there wasn't any Plan B.

Reluctantly, we reorganized things. One of our more palatial furnished downtown apartments had just come vacant. It was high in a secured building and had a well-policed underground garage. At three the next morning I moved in under another name. With Sonny around to sign for it I picked up an off-brand cell phone and used it exclusively to make short calls to our assistant in the office, Autherine, who could then relay whatever I needed to Buckley. Linda came by a couple of times a week for what I referred to as conjugal visits, which made her giggle.

Well into November the furor over Costa Rica kept blowing up in the newspapers, then subsiding for perhaps a week, then erupting into fresh incidents. On November 15 a drugged-up miner appeared on the plaza in front of the vast rectilinear City Hall in San Jose, lounged for hours around the big pink sculpture of a cow in front, then dragged an Uzi out of a brown paper bag and shot to death

Consuelo Raposa's Secretary of Commerce as he and his aide emerged through heavy, tinted-glass doors before the Civil Guardsman on duty could cut him down. Our conservative papers played the murder as another outrage by the leftist guerrillas openly taking over the Republic.

In fact the unassuming little Secretary came from the progressive wing of Raposa's party, and was an inveterate environmentalist. Here again, our editorial savants preached, a weak lady president dominated by radical advisors was permitting an important American partner in the Caribbean basin to succumb to anarchy and violence. That night a Monsanto seed storage facility burned to the ground. Special Operations Units in Miami, Panama and Tegucigalpa were put on alert.

CHAPTER XIII

Once Thanksgiving was in the offing I began to wonder whether we weren't overdoing my precautions. Apart from going stir-crazy and missing our profoundly gratifying, undeniably humdrum domestic existence on the Pink Streets, I had to wonder whether we might not be inflating this thing. After all, Murtha was one individual. It might make more sense to get more proactive. Smoke him out.

Then Dad called. He had been working up some statistics in the stacks at Southern Florida University of Tampa Bay when one of the interns brought in a portable phone. On it was Grover Stynehenge, who introduced himself with a recognizable burst of gusty, over-the-top enthusiasm. For more than thirty years he had been an insatiable goddamned reader of Dad's books and articles, a Sylvan Landau camp follower, you might put it. A couple of weeks ago the justice had enjoyed the distinct privilege of fraternizing – if that's the right word – with *young* Mr. Landau. An extremely penetrating legal mind, in the justice's view, understands how to support his case.

Promising as hell.

Dad thanked the justice.

One thing that happened was, young Michael indicated that we all lived in St. Petersburg. Which wasn't barely a stone's throw from where the justice and his wife Hasna liked to enjoy their leisure time. Nothing that fancy, this miniscule little spread on the edge of the Swamp with a couple of horses, just off the Myakka River. They would be down for the Thanksgiving break. Hasna – that's the wife – and Justice Stynehenge had the thought that maybe Dad and I and anybody else Dad would care to bring might like to stop by for a few hours toward the end of Thanksgiving afternoon. Have a drink. Did Dad drink?

Dad said he drank.

That was good news, Justice Stynehenge said. Maybe after we tipped a few Dad could get into the difference between a credit default swap and a derivative. Whatever the distinction was, the damned thing kept coming up in civil cases and still he really didn't have a clue. Would Saturday work? And forget Mr. Justice, Grover was just fine.

Dad said that he was honored, and took the number, and promised to get right back.

"I'd pass," Sonny recommended, when I told him about it. "How does that go, 'Welcome to my parlor, said the spider to the fly?' Murtha has his talents, but nobody ever accused him of subtlety. You have to assume he told Hasna to contact your father, and she conned Stynehenge into getting him down there."

"Dad wants to go. Stynehenge is one of his heroes.

He doesn't think anybody would try anything under the circumstances."

"He really doesn't think the guys attempting to murder Stynehenge on the installment plan would go after *you* out of respect for the majesty of the law? Your dad has been living in academia too long."

"Whatever anybody might try, Dad feels he could handle it," I said. "He's all in favor of bringing this thing to a head."

"And you think?"

"I'm torn. I do know another month of sardines on pita bread will probably leave me stark raving bonkers. And flatulent, beyond redemption. You won't want me around for your next venture into subversive diplomacy."

"You think it's my fault, this whole mess."

"There isn't anybody else to blame it on. Richard Nixon is dead."

Sonny passed a big, knobby hand through his wiry crest of hair. "Do whatever you need to do," he said slowly. "I'll try and back you up. Especially if you're the bait."

Justice Stynehenge had been right: His vest-pocket ranch wasn't that far from where we lived. It just took a full-time GPS specialist to locate the place. It wasn't one of mother's better days, so Dad and I set out in Dad's Avalon at three in the afternoon the Saturday after Thanksgiving expecting to arrive around four for early cocktails. We blew over the Sunshine Skyway bridge ahead of schedule and exited U.S. 75 on Fruitville Road headed east as per our Mapquest directions. Within a few miles we had left behind the outskirts of Sarasota, an exurban suburb with royal palms in the lane dividers and driving ranges and mortuaries and a Jehovah's Witness tabernacle behind a billboard that alerted us: "Jesus is coming. Are you ready?"

After that nothing jibed. This was farming country, with pastureland dominated by giant cylindrical bales, freshly rolled off the mowing machines and smelling of silage, and receding fields of Black Angus and Holsteins browsing. We did turn right on Verna Road and after that nothing accorded with our directions: byways and blocked outlets nowhere indicated in the Rand McNally atlas we brought as backup, packed dirt turn-offs and pavement obviously headed the wrong way.

By then we were late. Stynehenge had supplied us with his unlisted number; I called that on my cell phone. Some sort of hired man answered. He told us to get back to the Verna Road junction and he would meet us there and lead us to Last Chance Ranch, which was what Justice Stynehenge called his spread.

It took maybe five minutes before Stynehenge's caretaker showed up. A small, pouchy senior, he instructed us to follow his banged-up pickup truck. "I got these cataracts," he told us. "You don't want to follow too close. These roads here goes every whichaway, nothin' but cow-paths, basically."

Stynehenge was waiting in his dooryard, on two canes, pale locks tangled around the neckline of his short-sleeved shirt, attempting to quiet down a big patchy-looking yellow dog. The dog was alternately leaping and scrounging its belly against the dirt. Beyond a split-rail fence, two horses were champing up what grass there was.

"Tracked me to my hideout!" Stynehenge exclaimed. "For years we had Secret Service surveillance, but even the local cokeheads finally figured out there wasn't a whole lot to break in for. Now I depend on Bartlett here and his shotgun to keep the peace."

"Except I can't shoot straight no more counta the cataracts," Bartlett said.

"They don't know that," Stynehenge said. "You two better come inside with me and have a drink."

As advertised, the farmhouse was unpretentious. It was a sizeable one-story building, barn-red, sheathed to the soffits in novelty siding, which was beginning to peel. Gravely, protectively, the big yellow dog plodded in ahead of Stynehenge.

There was a veranda on two sides, which opened through French doors into a long living room. At one end a fire was burning down to embers in a walk-in fireplace faced with landon stone. Four wing-back chairs were arrayed around a plank coffee table.

"Take a seat," Stynehenge directed us. "Hasna is doin' the honors in the kitchen. We keep it simple. What can I get you to drink?"

Swinging with some difficulty above the canes, Stynehenge made his way to the bar beside the door to the kitchen and came up with a couple of gins and tonic and the predictable double vodka. Hasna, in an apron, bustled in carrying a tray of a cream-cheese hors d'oeuvres she called struki. One fell off the tray and seemed to bounce off the hooked rug into the jaws of the big yellow dog. He crunched it down very noisily, slobbering with pleasure.

"Hopalong loves his victuals," Stynehenge told us. "Getting' to be an old hound. Misses us something terrible, Bartlett says, so he goes halfway bananas every time we make it down."

Dad took a struki. Justice Stynehenge slugged off an inch of his vodka. "I dug out your book about Joe Schumpeter last night and read until my eyes gave out," the justice told Dad. "Made even more sense than when I read it the first time. Where do you think we are today? Do you at this stage go along with the concept that predatory capitalism in its exaggerated current form is really going to bring down some kind of corporate socialism liable to extinguish entrepreneurship once and for all? Do you...."

Once Stynehenge opened up, the cowboy populist receded and the academic jurist who had been widely respected before he ever ascended to the federal bench kept coming through. Dad's energy levels rose. I knew that he had boned up on the credit default swap/derivatives issue; Lefty never seemed to get around to that. Outside the tall windows at both ends of the long room dark had started falling.

I couldn't help letting my mind wander from time to time. The big room was barely decorated – a bald eagle, pinions outstretched for perhaps seven feet, hung from the ceiling on nylon cables above us. A ceiling fan with vast woven-raffia blades. In one corner a stuffed panther had been mounted so as to rear up, claws open. There were Western engravings above the wainscoting.

Dusk was settling in outside. The land fell off and I could see the descending ridge of the blackened tree-line. I had to fight the suspicion that somebody was out there, probably several people. After half an hour Stynehenge stopped speaking in mid-sentence and minced his lips; I could see – and smell – that he had lost bladder control. His crotch was darkening. As if on cue, Hasna filled the doorway and stepped forcefully over the dog. "Grover needs time out," she announced, reaching under his arms to boost him up onto his canes. "He don't want nobody to help him sometimes, he got good life still, but now we give him medicine break."

Guided and supported, Stynehenge wobbled toward the other rear door and into the back. Dad started to say something, then couldn't. He took a heavy breath. "I guess I left my shoulder pack in the car," Dad muttered, mostly to himself. "Another dummkopf move. Getting old." The yellow dog, which appeared to have fallen asleep sitting up with its muzzle on Dad's knee, came to and stared longingly into Dad's eyes.

"You've made another conquest," I said. "You can't be stopped."

After twenty minutes Lefty reappeared. Dad stood up. "Maybe we should—"

"No, no," Justice Stynehenge was vehement. "Mid-afternoon slump. Happens every once in a while." He produced an enormous grin, protruding a badly yellowed upper and lower plate. "Hasna here takes care of me, and I am now *totally rejuvenated.*"

Lefty let himself down into his wing chair. Hasna left to bring in supper on a tray – salad, a loaf of soggy dark bread, several skewers of grilled minced nuggets of meat the name of which she spelled out for us – cevapcici, che-

vop-che-che – once we moved over and we settled in around the table. Everything did taste delicious. There was a very sweet pastry afterwards, like a baklava.

Stynehenge ate very slowly. We lapsed into small talk. Dad admired the stuffed panther. Hasna explained proudly that Grover had shot the animal years before – several marriages before, in fact, although Hasna left that out. The panther had gone after one of the horses.

Somebody mentioned a couple of new films expected over the holidays. Lefty hinted that I would like the decision when the Supreme Court issued its next batch of opinions. We tried to handicap the upcoming Congressional elections. Stynehenge was attempting to lead the conversation; abruptly, after a couple of minutes, he was wilting again. Every once in a while he seemed to blanch, and gag a little to gulp in air through his open mouth, as if he were fighting nausea.

Lefty did keep at the vodka. Once we had eaten Dad and I stood up to leave. Stynehenge, obviously exerting himself, rocked along a little blearily on the two canes as he conducted us to the door, followed slavishly by Hopalong. The big yellow dog stayed with us, watching and wheezing affectionately as we said goodbye before climbing into Dad's Avalon. I would be driving. Hasna provided me a little penciled-in strip map indicating the turns to get us back onto Fruitville Road.

The dog rubbed up against Dad; then, without any warning, Hopalong began to sound off, a sharp urgent belling the animal would not give up on even as we swung out of the dooryard and started to head west through the dark. I could still hear him yowling when I picked up on the headlights of another car following me as I negotiated the turns.

"Hopalong is lovelorn," I said to Dad.

"Either that or he knows something we don't." The car behind us had started to close the gap. "We better get back on one of the main roads," Dad said. He'd pulled his shoulder pack into his lap in the passenger seat.

By now Hasna's strip map wasn't of any use – we'd taken too many unmarked turns. But we had blundered onto something that resembled a Class-A highway marked by a yellow Florida Department of Transportation shield with a heavy curved arrow and the inscription MYAKKA Something – I didn't have time enough read it all. I slowed down a second or two to check the oncoming so we didn't burst onto the highway and get T-boned but then the car behind us banged our bumper hard, jolting us forward. "They're trying to force us off the road," I said to Dad. Reflection off the headlights of another car, far behind, glistened in the foliage. "I'm going to floor it."

I hung a left and the Avalon torqued up. We opened the gap for a mile or so but then our pursuers closed the interval. There was a sharp bend and for a few moments we were out of range of their headlights and I caught sight of a stoned-in planter on the left and the image of a wary stork waving its orange beak above MYAKKA RIVER STATE PARK. I had turned off before I really registered onto a winding access road lighted by a big late-harvest moon and overhung all the way in by an archway of black, dying oaks which trailed their Spanish moss low enough to brush the pavement, a cathedral of decay.

Whoever was after us was directly behind us. I

gunned it past the Ranger Station and the Canopy Walkway but the road ended in an expanse of empty parking lots and what looked like darkened W.P.A. exhibition buildings designated Myakka Outpost and Tram and Airboat Ticket Booth. "We'll probably do better on foot," Dad said. His shoulder pack was open. "I've got my Beretta." He'd geared down into that resolute, unflappable state genuine danger provoked in him, Dad's Viet-Nam-Combat persona, so different from his academic whimsicality, his congenital ebullience in the face of a troubled world.

Dad grabbed a flashlight and we abandoned the locked Avalon next to the stanchion of a towering florescent arc lamp and ducked behind a souvenir hut and onto a path. Behind us a car door slammed. We pushed on through a stand of stunted pine and outstretched pineapple palms that lashed our faces toward what either of us could really more sense than see in the mottled moonlight was some kind of standing water. You could inhale it, a fetid green stench.

Plunging into shadow, we stalled just long enough to catch a glimpse of our pursuers. Murtha was unmistakable – square-set, limping into the dark in the direction we'd gone. The younger man with him was taller, raw-boned, and as suddenly he passed through a bar of dusty forest light I spotted the forelock bobbing against his temple and realized who that was – the waiter at the Cosmos Club! We'd been under surveillance, even at that table!

One of them spotted us; we hurtled on deeper towards the water and virtually without a sound, terrifyingly, an upflux of dozens and dozens of big, very dark nesting birds rose around us in every direction. "Stay away from those bastardly things," Dad husked out. "Black vultures! I remember in Nam! Those fuckers eat anything, they'll peck the rubber out from around your windshield, they like to go for your eyes--"

There was what looked like a kind of deteriorated concrete barrier that formed the junction with a river to our left fed by the open water we could now see clearly ahead of us: a placid lake glimmering under the moon around an island of water hyacinths. We scrambled onto the barrier. Halfway across the cracked, treacherous ridge of the dam we both sensed the bank of the river to our left starting to come alive. Several pairs of alligators, each at least twelve feet long, were pushing through the mud to cut us off before we could clamber back out onto solid ground. There was a stand of mature live oak silhouetted against the lake beyond and without a word we made for that. Alligators can move very fast on mud, we heard their tails slapping as we double-timed toward the trees, and somehow both of us broke into the thicket seconds before those monsters arrived so we could drag each other up onto a thick lower bough.

Dad was a little out of breath. "I liked meeting Stynehenge," he got out, "but by and large I think your social life needs a lot of work."

"I told you there was risk."

"Risk of getting shot, maybe. But never eaten. I've really never wanted to get eaten, that is where I have to draw the line with you, Michael."

"Your standards are very high."

Murtha and the waiter must have gotten close enough to get a look at the alligators. Finally, through the trees that abutted the souvenir shop, I heard a car start up and drive off. Cautiously, I withdrew my cell phone from a trouser pocket and punched in Sonny's number.

"And you are where?" I wanted to know. "The world's greatest tracker?"

"Crisscrossing this godforsaken wasteland between pastures. What happened? Did you turn off someplace? How we going to trap Murtha if nobody can find anybody?"

I told him where we were. Any thought of entrapping Murtha was out for the night. Below our dangling feet – not that far below our dangling feet – at least a half dozen alligators were fanned out. Dad kept a pocket-light in his shoulder pack. Once in a while he played a beam across their corrugated, gunmetal backs and spiked tails. Several raised their snouts. Their unblinking ruby eye-shine scintillated in the patchy moonlight – prehistoric flesh-eaters, accustomed to waiting out prey.

"No point in shooting the bastards," Dad said. "In any case, I wouldn't know which part to shoot."

After what seemed a very long time I heard a vehicle pull into the parking lot, circle, brake where the Avalon was parked. I shouted. Sonny gave us a whoop. There was enough visibility through the intersecting boughs for me to make out his angular frame as he picked his way across the dam and through the swampy underbrush. He had a long, black utility flashlight of the sort cops use like a mace, with a hemisphere around the bulb. The moment he burst into the trees he started swinging the big light wildly, then held it under his face and raised his other arm above his head, fluttering his powerful fingers.

Beneath us there was a rippling stir and the giant reptiles pulled closer to the trunk of our tree. A couple of them bellowed; the thick, musky odor they sprayed contaminated the swampy air as they hunched up and started to slither away in all directions. We waited perhaps a minute before we could make ourselves hang from the bough a moment, then drop.

"About ready to leave?" Sonny wanted to know. "Alligators panic when they think they're about to go against something bigger than they are. That's why you want to get your arms up. What brain they've got is about the size of a walnut. Somewhere underneath the plate behind their eyes."

"And where did that come from?" I asked.

"Your, uh—Linda's last husband? Savage Owl – Charlie. He wrestled alligators for a living for a while. Sometimes he let me help. You don't want to let them get too comfortable with people. Tourists around the park here probably toss them twinkies and crap like that and get too close so relatives can snap some pictures. The gators get conditioned to the scent of humans, and the next thing you know some toddler and his plastic truck get pulled under and squirreled away in one of their nests for lunch. They'll eat it all, even the truck. The thing you don't want----"

Sonny was nerved up, rattling on to ground himself. But Dad and I weren't over it yet, certainly not into conversation, and Sonny saw that. "Probably time to close the Nature Park," he decided.

Back in the parking lot Sonny checked the undercarriage of Dad's Avalon to make sure Murtha hadn't installed a car bomb. Nobody had slashed the tires, or even let the air out. "They may have left it to the 'gators to take care of you," Sonny said. "Or else they may have figured you were likely to make it out of there before long and they'd be waiting someplace on the road. You better go out ahead and I'll follow close in the Equinox. They'll probably give it up for tonight when they see you've got backup."

We said that would be appreciated.

CHAPTER XIV

Somehow our adventure in the Swamp left me more unfulfilled than intimidated. I still needed to do something to bring this whole business to a head. Then I thought of Freddy Wilmot at the *Miami Post-Dispatch.*

I remembered that Sonny had mentioned that publicity could generate the blowback in touchy situations when nothing else worked. Without access to the *Post-Dispatch*'s morgue of leads and clippings about the Cuban-American financier Ramon Perez y Cruz, our sister Wendy's father-in-law, we would never have understood the danger we were in early enough to protect ourselves. If Freddy Wilmot still worked at the paper, maybe he could help.

I called Freddy from a pay-phone and explained exactly who and what we needed to know about. Around four the next morning I emerged from the underground garage of our building, headed north on our seemingly deserted turnpike in my aging BMW, merged onto U.S. 4, and exited outside Daytona to gas up and eat lunch. Nobody was on my tail.

In Miami I parked in a lot and grabbed a cab for

Dispatch Plaza – most likely an unnecessary precaution. Security in the main building had my name on the check list. One of the guards walked me back to Freddy Wilmot's cubicle.

Wilmot did look scruffy – older, balder, more disgruntled than ever. I had begun to suspect that this was mostly his act – when people felt sorry for Freddy they tended to talk freely. Stories under his byline kept popping up in national syndication.

Very little had changed. He had another ficus, which was going brown around the edges. I took the worn old oak swivel chair Freddy kept pulled out for visitors. "Weren't you the has-been who assured me you were about to retire four years ago?" I opened.

"I did retire. Then I got a dog. Then the dog contracted fleas. Then I contracted fleas. Then I had the dog put down. I was bored. I told the vet I'd slip him an extra grand if he'd put me down, but he seemed to have a problem with that. Then I came back here and they were fucked-up enough to take me on again. The adolescent ditzes they keep on hiring can't write, they have no story sense, none of them have a clue when it comes to tracking down a lead. So here I am. They even pay me once in a while." He pulled on his twisted orange nose. "Nothing has really changed, except I lost a lung."

"Cancer?"

"Athlete's foot. What do you think?"

"Sorry to hear that."

"So was I. It was definitely a setback. Chemo was a bitch. Odd thing is, now that I got some energy back I keep getting the feeling there is still one real big story out there with my name on it. Just waitin' for me to jump its bones. Crazy, no? How's Dad? The Adam Smith book still selling?"

"Gangbusters. They're still lining up all the way around the block."

Wilmot gave me a look. "I don't remember you as such a wiseass." He retrieved an electronic cigarette out of his desk drawer and drew thoughtfully on it, so that the tip glowed. "It ain't the same," Freddy Wilmot said. "I miss those coffin nails."

I cocked my chair back. "Anything on your screen vis-a-vis the two I mentioned yesterday?"

"Some." Wilmot held up a sheaf if printouts. "More than I thought there'd be. Especially Mr. Murtha. You did yourself a favor remembering him as Generoso Sanchez. He popped his cherry in the Agency under that name. We had a guy here picked up a Pulitzer following that sonovabitch around during the Iran-Contra dustup. Spoke fluent Spanish, handy as hell."

Freddy Wilmot coughed. "Force of habit," he explained. "Even with this worthless frigging piece of crap." He emitted a puff of steam and put down the electronic cigarette. "For about a year Generoso was the last government employee any of our guys could identify when it came to payoffs. He ran the gonzos set off those firecracker mines in Managua harbor that pissed off Barry Goldwater. The Contras pick up a couple of Cuban advisors to the Sandinistas, and who do you suppose winds up on film in a *Newsweek* photospread directing the desperate little fucks while they are digging their own graves and laying –lying? -- down in the holes waiting to get their throats cut? We found out later it was Sanchez spread the bucks around when CIA peppered the bureaucracy in San Jose with stoolies."

"I heard something about that," I said.

"Our reporter figured Sanchez must have *wanted* the publicity. He gets quite forthright, especially after a few pops. Treated it like-- learning the tools of his trade. Tough, your go-to guy!"

"But when did anybody lose track of him?"

"He's in and out," Freddy Wilmot said. "We have no idea when he got religion and turned into Staniford Murtha. I heard he married some piece of English trim, social aspirations somebody said. Jesus! Our reporter spotted him on the ground in Srebrenica a couple of days before it really hit the fan *there*. We assume he's free lance now – some kind of contractor. Something here about Libya – probably a rumor." Wilmot put the paperwork down. "Now, how did you--?"

"Sort of a social engagement. We met in San Jose."

"Which leaves us where?" Wilmot took a long pull on his fake cigarette, which glowed hard. "I take it he's not going to marry one of your other sisters—"

"Now, there's an appetizing thought," I said. "Still -- maybe that would work. Might get him to leave me alone."

"When do we get to that part?" Wilmot said. "Why would he fuck around with you?"

"It's a tangled web," I said. "I met him pretty much by accident in Costa Rica—"

"Recently? Before or after the shit started to hit the fan?" I could literally see Wilmot's newsman's ears starting to prick up. "You're telling me he might be underneath something like that?"

"Could be," I said. I really didn't want to implicate Sonny. "The time I met Murtha I was sort of..of incognito. You know how San Jose is, a bordello on every street corner? I was on vacation, by myself. Murtha was into the booze, and he started sounding off about what he and the Canadian mining interests he and -- get this! – his sponsor our vice president Alvin Scheel had in mind once they were able to confirm metallurgical reports that the palladium and especially the rhodium deposits they were after were under the mountains around Abangares. North of San Jose."

I laid out pretty much everything Sonny and I had picked up eves-dropping on Murtha and Audrey – the propaganda campaign, the paramilitary apes from Honduras scheduled to sneak in and tear half of Costa Rica to pieces, the heavy money already in the pipeline to sway conservative politicians.

"I guess I really didn't think about it all that much at the time," I told Wilmot, reddening in spite of myself as it came to me how many lies it was taking to cover my ass properly. "Murtha basically struck me as, you know, another over-the-hill veteran laying on the bullshit while he was getting plowed. But then I happened to run into him again a couple of weeks afterwards in D.C.

"It happens that Justice Grover Stynehenge is a great fan of my father, like you, and I was in town on a case and Lefty invited me to dinner at his club. While I was walking in I spotted Murtha slipping an envelope that looked to me as if it could be stuffed with currency to Justice Stynehenge's latest wife, Hasna. The next day Murtha almost managed to stick a knife into me in the D.C. Metro.

He has been on my case ever since. I'd obviously seen too much – probably involved that woman."

"Lefty's wife? And the connection is--?"

"It happens – pure coincidence – that a relative of our family is clerking for the justice. She's suspicious. Stynehenge has raging rheumatoid arthritis, and the new wife administers his injections. They tell me one dose too many at the wrong time could finish the old guy."

"Holy shit," Freddy Wilmot said. "Wouldn't that be a lulu? Especially with the war powers case coming up, and him the swing vote."

"Anything turn up related to her?"

"Not really a hellova lot. She showed up in this country around 2000, we took in a number of those buggers under CIA auspices right after the deal went down. Sort of a sop Richard Holbrooke threw to the Serbs to bring off the Dayton Accords, help out the families of the implicated. Her father's brother was Anton Prokic, ran more than his share of extremely bloody errands for Milosevic. His performance in Srebrenica left him with the World Court pushing hard to track him down."

"What do we know about her politics?"

"Zilch. She had enough of a medical background to put in months in one of the Belgrade hospitals when Clinton was bombing the shit out of the place. Worked for a while in New Jersey and after that got some training as a practical nurse in Georgetown. We got our hands on a police report that escaped the shredder which made it clear she was not above trafficking in medical morphine when she could get her hands on it. Nobody attempted to prefer charges for quite a while. The doctors liked having her around -- sucks a mean dick, according to our informant."

"But then I gather Hasna moved on?" I was struggling to keep my voice down: too much fit.

"The thing is, she got kind of in and out. Shows up for work for a while, and then she's liable to go missing for maybe a month. Could be she was still at Georgetown when Murtha got his initial whiff. Picked up on something he liked. I doubt it went all the way back to Srebrenica, although it could have. Those Agency fuckers would bird-dog a sniff of pussy they can use through the jaws of Hades, literally. We recognize the pattern, we see it all the time with assets CIA is developing."

"So you think – hooking up with Lefty Stynehenge might have been—"

"Maybe it was true romance. Maybe it was on the way to a very inviting paycheck."

"In a way I wish I hadn't asked." The rush from details this raw was leaving my mouth dry. "What can anybody do?"

"More than you'd think. I know a couple of guys who feed the tabloids. Carnivores, basically, liable to slant this thing any fucking way, but what you want is attention, am I correct? A hint here, the right name dropped there, some hacker to resuscitate the deleted files they need out of the District of Columbia police archives....This thing could spread, go big-time in a couple of news cycles. Just let me run with it." Milky as they were, Freddy Wilmot's eyes had started to sparkle. "We've got a goddamn fucking *monster* of a back story here, you ought to know that, and with what you told me there's plenty to get started on."

"I guess you're right," I said. "All I'm basically

concerned with is keeping Costa Rica quiet and Lefty Stynehenge alive. Along with myself. Murtha showed up in Florida last week and almost fed Sylvan and me to a pack of alligators. I'm hiding out, most of the time."

"I'd say it's time to take the fight to those motherfuckers directly, wouldn't you think? We do it all the time – politicians and other types of criminals go after our reporters every day. You got to hit back harder, first." Wilmot tossed me a heavy, professional wink. "Whatever happens, I really wouldn't worry too much. Lawyers are expendable."

I'd had no idea how fast national publicity could flare up and explode until Freddy Wilmot went to work. Within forty-eight hours there was an item in *The Haughtington Post*'s The National Speculum column: "**Vice President Alvin Sheel:** "Sources privy to the blind trust of our ingenious vice president assure this correspondent that within the last three months trustees have tripled Mr. Sheel's already substantial position in the international resource miner Coyote Creek Resources. For years lawyers for Coyote Creek have been contesting claims by Costa Rican government officials that options on mineral rights its predecessor corporation negotiated sixty years ago and continued to treat as open-ended have in fact long since expired. With political trouble brewing in the doughty, left-leaning little Republic, and U.S. interests purportedly at risk, it is a chore for this column not to speculate as to whether the incessantly maneuvering vice president might not know something about those leases the rest of us will only find out once it's too late."

Across the more traditional press the brouhaha in Costa Rica was rousing ever sharper responses. The Hard Right outlets were getting more distraught every day by each reported bombing, the repeated waves of student demonstrators in San Jose and Puntarenas ranting against any threatened intervention by the ever-predatory Colossus of the North.

Gravely, the editorial page deacons of *The Manhattan Times* cautioned Madame President Arosa about the long-term consequences of inviting into her fragile democracy hardened military personnel from authoritarian societies like Venezuela and Bolivia and Cuba, too often utterly ruthless security cadre, bitter junta veterans. It would be the naïve and freedom-loving Ticos, the *Times* warned, who in all probability would wind up cowering in their basements if and when the United States found itself obliged to save them. Panama still hadn't recovered.

Yet within days an alternative reading of events had begun to seep into the national coverage. A Tegucigalpa-based stringer for the left-leaning U.S. weekly *Our Republic* followed up on rumors sweeping the Honduran capital that one of the insurgents implicated in blowing up a wing of the Apartamento Montaverde assisted living complex above San Jose was actually Honduran military. Too close to the blast, he'd made it back when fellow squad members insisted on exfiltrating him; now, beginning to recover some hearing and traumatically burned over eighty percent of his legs and trunk, he was recuperating in a military hospital outside Tegucigalpa attached to Soto Cano air base.

Soto Cano – Palmerola to the gringos – housed U.S. Joint Task Force Bravo, five to six hundred American trainers and pilots with Chinook and Black Hawk units whose purported mission was to support Honduran army elements scouring the jungles to expedite the war on drugs. Word around the capital was that most of the paramilitaries the U.S. was backing up worked largely in the agricultural hinterlands, discouraging insubordinate peasants. Blatantly out of uniform, drawn predominantly from clustered wattle villages of Mayan near-aborigines along the Mosquito Coast, these irregulars were mostly sent in to intimidate -- often kidnap, sometime "disappear" – home-grown protesters and would-be union organizers.

They targeted whatever loudmouths threatened to disrupt the palm oil plantations installed by Consolidated Brands. During one insurrection government-backed gunmen reportedly cornered nine activists and "cooked them to death in bread ovens." Consolidated Brands was the successor entity to Consolidated Fruit, the legendary U.S. corporation behind a string of banana republics.

As recently as the Reagan years, the enforcement of acceptable labor practices had been left up to the notorious Battalion 316. Now, these stepchildren of the Honduran military were available for special assignment. The afternoon the stringer from *Our Republic* was able to bribe his way into the military hospital in the Soto Cano base he found the blast victim getting his wet packs changed. Judging from what little skin was untreated around his jaw-line and temples the patient was clearly a Mosquito Indian, barely able to get out enough pidgin Spanish to make himself understood. The stringer shouted questions at him;

badly frightened still, yet indignant that he had very nearly been left behind after setting off a faulty detonator by a team leader who *expected* him to get blown up, the patient was frantic. Blinking incessantly through blistered eyelids, he did not seem to care who heard or what happened afterwards.

He was prepared to tell everything. He and his team had been pulled off a harassment project in one of the cooperatives in the Aguan River basin. They were to be smuggled into Costa Rica after a sea trip around the Caribbean coast of Nicaragua. They moved at night, hauling their own explosives. Only the team leader had the map with the targets. All that the men were told was that this was a revenge for two hundred years of abuses by the Norteamericanos.

This was a totally different take on Costa Rica from the home-grown/left-wing-terrorist scenario most of the press here had been propagating. The story the stringer sent in, compressed into two columns in the little weekly's Screams and Portents section, would under normal circumstances have been dismissed by establishment media as another hysterical bleat from the infatuated left and ignored. Except that hard-right radio talk show host Rodney – "the Rodent" – Lansdale stumbled on the report and obsessed for two straight days about the nest of "Soviet-inspired traitors poisoning the very air we breathe from the scumbag editorial premises of journalistic toilets like *Our Republic*."

With that, indignation arced to several militantly reactionary papers, then to conservative television outlets, where the story was noisily ridiculed on the Sunday panel shows. A recently retired CIA case officer, who had just come out with a book cautiously jaundiced in his appraisal of a number of his Agency superiors, was interviewed on a cable channel. Yes, he was frank to concede elements of the *Our Republic* shocker . We did at times employ native militias to help keep the peace around much of Central America. This could involve favors to the important plantation owners. Use irregulars as mercenaries to destabilize a nearby nation? These things were known to happen, sadly, yes.

With that the *Manhattan Times* readdressed the upheaval in Costa Rica in a follow-up editorial. Perhaps a moment of judicious reconsideration *was* indicated here. Whatever the bottom line in this unfortunate turn of events in Central America, restraint ought to be our hallmark before we indulged yet another time our addiction to "covert global miniwars." Other nations in the region were concerned, and in several cases had already pledged troops to shore up Madame President Raposa. Perhaps *they* might quiet things down. These flare-ups could quickly become expensive, and the populations for which we sacrificed our blood and treasure so often ultimately turned on *us*. At the absolute minimum it might well be prudent to delay military involvement until after the Supreme Court has ruled on the War Powers Act.

CHAPTER XV

The morning the *Times* genteely reversed its position I got a call on my backup cell phone from Freddie Wilmot. I was still in and out of hiding, the subject of my own cockamamie Witness Protection Program. At unexpected moments I had started dropping by our law office, then out the back before surveillance could get itself organized.

Or so I hoped. Murtha was going to find me, that I knew. When that happened, who would have the drop on who? Whom? I needed to make this happen as soon as possible. He could take his time.

Meanwhile, the arguments before the Supremes in re the War Powers Resolution were expected to go before the Court the last week before the Christmas recess. The case was then scheduled to go to conference right after the first of the year. If Murtha and Alvin Sheel expected to strong-arm the reluctant Congress into moving on Costa Rica based on no more than a last-minute resolution based on vague, increasingly controversial "police powers," they had the rest of the year to put the pressure on.

Once the High Court decided that engaging troops

overseas would once again require a formal declaration of war by the Congress as stipulated in Article One of the Constitution, far fewer of the legislators were likely to go on record as supporting this incursion. The implications of the report in *Our Republic* were sinking in around Capitol Hill. A majority to invade would probably be impossible to get.

The Freddie Wilmot who called me the morning the second *Times* editorial hit was somebody I had never met. Wilmot always seemed to style himself as resolutely over-the-hill, a professional burnout, cynical, blase. The man I talked with that day was a cub reporter crowing about his scoop, the stripling who bagged the mastodon with a sharp stick. "I gotta tell you Mike this is very spectacular for me," Freddie opened. "How often in a career does this happen, the powers that be hit the brake and wham the country swivels around? On a dime! You saw *The Manhattan Times* today?"

"I did."

"That is your accomplishment, dollink. You put it all together and history is being made. Really, history is being made!"

"It's been a barrage," I had to concede. "You laid the whole thing down."

"You gave me the coordinates. Christ, what a moment. 'Rumors sweeping the Honduran capital' – what a crock that was! We had our guy in Guatemala City catch the connecting flight down and put a big bad bee in the ear of that graduate student *Our Republic* likes to refer to as a stringer. Everything you told me. That was what kicked it off, I hope you realize.

"I still can not fucking believe this thing. *The Manhattan Times*! The Great Grey Lady of the American Establishment hikes up her skirts and shows the world her petootie! When did that ever happen before? What's next, the JFK assassination?"

"People forget pretty fast," I said. "By the first of the February all this could very well blow over and Marines could be leading Madame Arosa away at gunpoint."

"Could happen," Wilmot said. There was a pause. "That's why I called." An uncharacteristic hesitancy was creeping into Wilmot's delivery. "I got to tell you, what this story needs in a voice. A face. Somebody willing to stand up and lay it all out first hand – this happened to me—"

I cut him off. "I see where you're headed," I said. "I'm not by nature exactly a stand-up type. I'm basically a lawyer. I step in while the dust is settling and pick up the pieces—"

"Normally, maybe. At this point you're a player whether you like it or no. You put these Agency bastards under the lights you'll see them scatter like cucarachas. Otherwise, before a hellova lot longer, the way they think they take you out of the picture. Murtha is the first wave. We cover reluctant witnesses all the time. Once things start heating up it gets to be: Testify or die."

I don't think I have ever been more conflicted. I hated the idea, but how else to back off Murtha? "How would this work, specifically?" I responded, after a long moment.

"That part I could arrange," Freddie Wilmot said. "I worked over the years with a producer at The Liberation

Channel, which is very hot, who I would judge has the cajones for an interview like this. After this week Costa Rica is going to light up, priority coverage, controversial, I understand 20-20 is planning a segment. You need to go up to New York and tell the country what you told me."

"You think that really would help?"

"Has to take the heat off. Why would they bother to dust you after that?"

'I guess I'm likely to find out," I said.

I was in a quandary. Before I was willing to give Wilmot the go-ahead I wanted a lot more orientation. Sonny was between exams. We arranged to get together at one of the picnic tables off the fishing pier at Bay Vista Park, around four. Except for the horde of hungry pelicans waiting for the late-afternoon fishermen to arrive and toss them entrails , the place was likely to be deserted. We could see anybody approaching through the surrounding pines or turning into the big stretch of patchy, fissured pavement off Fourth Avenue.

"Wilmot could be right," Sonny agreed after I went over the onslaught of media Freddie had set loose. "Sunlight, I told you that could make a difference. We redskins are very publicity-averse, and underneath all that bushwa about status Murtha is probably like the rest of us. Hates mirrors, doesn't like his picture taken. No doubt cowers inside when anybody steps on his shadow. It's like somebody stepped on our soul. Remember I told you the sonovabitch started life as a Pima Indian? Generoso Sanchez? Even Sanchez was probably something his people picked up to hide their origins in one of those mud-

and- thatch pole huts along the Salt River."

"I'll try not to step on his shadow," I said. "What else should I know?"

"I think I went into most of this before. Just remember that Murtha is essentially a free-lance at this stage. A contract player. He needs money, he needs backing, and you can be sure that, if he really is forerunning this Costa Rica subversion program on Alvin Sheel's dollar, Sheel and those creeps over there in Blair House are not going to go along if anything threatens to splash back on them."

"You're saying – don't push it?"

"No, no. Are you listening? I'm saying – you *have* to push it. You're in too deep. Murtha obviously thinks he can maybe cover his tracks by taking you out. The more people understand about what's going on, the less difference it's going to make whether you are in the picture or not. Also, the less incentive Murtha has to stick around here and waste the few days he has left before the Supreme Court decides."

"That could be," I said. "It just doesn't seem to me Murtha is the type to deal in subtleties."

"This ain't subtle. It's routine bureaucratic boilerplate. Sheel and whoever is coordinating all this around the Agency will not want to deal with anything too explicit, like you getting blown away the day after showing up front and center on some national interview. It's all about compartmentation with those buggers. Deniability. They've never gotten over their attempts to pass off Jack Ruby as a 'police character.'"

"Only you," I said. "You're saying I've got to stick my neck out to keep my head from being chopped off."

"You're saying it. I'm only corroborating it."

"Anything else? I could use some ideas."

"Well – I liked the way you tried to bait Murtha into making his move at Stynehenge's hacienda down there. Not a total success, but at least you showed the flag. Now you know he's pretty much operating by himself."

"Except for the waiter."

"That's one individual, not a swat team." Sonny folded his long, sinewy forearms in front of himself and cocked his blade of a jaw. "How about you pull together some troops of your own? Maybe that Cuban brother-in-law, the SEAL. Don't they usually show up around Christmas?"

"Rickey? I hate to ask."

"Ask. Wasn't he the hombre that cold-cocked those brothers that had a contract on you and Sylvan at that airboat place?"

"The Parcados, right."

"Ricky is probably itching for a little action. Suppose you move him in over the holidays? He gets to sit around on your front stoop or whatever that thing is called cleaning his AK 47. Protect the family. Murtha would get the message."

"I guess," I said. "I sure as hell would like to sleep in my own bed again. Rick could have the other bunk in Ten Bears' room. Ten Bears would love that."

"So your problems are solved," Sonny said. "See, in the end you'll probably wind up with the Citizen's Medal or the Good Housekeeping Seal of Approval or some such overdue honor. Consuela Arosa will embrace you at the United Nations. You will thank me for introducing you to

Big Stan Murtha."

"Funny you should mention that. Deep down," I said, "I've been grateful all along."

My burly Cuban-American brother-in-law, Enrique Perez y Cruz, ex-SEAL and fledgling financier, moved in the week before Christmas. "Wendy prefer me to be home at the holidays," Rick explained as he was unpacking his rucksack. "But I explain, listen, love bucket, blood is thicker than water." He pronounced it, blawd ees theeker than *wad*-er. "When I tell her what happen, how some guys trying to off you, she say you got to go. Everybody need Mike."

"That's reassuring," I said. "I hoped I fit in somewhere."

Rick draped a bicep like a melon onto one of my narrow shoulders and gave me a hug. "Nobody want to underestimate you, compadre," he said. "We learn that the other time."

"I think we all just needed to get used to one another," I said.

Making love with Linda was different at home. While I was lying over in the condominium things tended to get rushed. She had to get back to Ten Bears and I needed my sleep. One felt the pressure from the management, even though I was the management.

At home one thing lead of itself to another. Linda had a way of undressing as if she were opening up the secret gift I had been hinting about for a long, long time. When she was wearing a bra she undid herself cup by cup, never in a hurry, as if she were about to present fruit. As her panties came off her gaze softened: She was liberating herself. Even before she even made it into bed I invariably started thickening, fore and aft.

I needed to survive. On edge this way, day after day, I realized my life effectively began the night Linda fed me peyote and took me in under the buffalo robe. She knew we were under siege and that I needed a lot of support. I couldn't really accommodate panic.

The weeks of crisis over Costa Rica were obviously coming up, and now I had to assume some sort of public role. A week or so before Christmas I got a call on my backup cell phone from Chris Nugent, a producer at The Liberation Channel. If I was up for it he'd laid on a half-hour interview in prime time with Daniel Prosper, the uninhibited, old-line anchorman whose integrity had gotten him bumped from network to network until he landed on the Liberation Channel, where anybody could say anything.

This was important stuff: The channel intended to flag the announcement throughout the week leading up to the interview itself. They needed a minute or so of comment from me, on tape, that they could run as a sort of preliminary trailer to pump up viewership. Would I be willing to tape such a thing in Tampa at a public station on Martin Luther King, Jr. Boulevard?

I said I would. Nugent said that he had already penciled me in for the ultimate interview, live, with Dan Prosper in their New York City home studio. Scheduled for one P.M., the Tuesday after Christmas, then rerun several times on successive evenings. On Friday of the following week the Supreme Court would announce its momentous War Powers decision. With Costa Rica heating up, and all the attention the high court was attracting just then, my contribution couldn't sync in better.

The news breaks Freddie Wilmot continued to plant and all that focus on the Supreme Court just then were triggering secondary explosions. Ten days before Christmas a bombshell hit the popular media with the appearance of the December 20 issue of the supermarket tabloid *The Federal Investigator*. Its glossy cover highlighted a very unflattering image of Justice Stynehenge, collapsed against his scooter, face thrown back, his thin, white Kit Carson locks a dirty fringe around his hollow neck, gasping hard to breathe through his withered rictus of a mouth. He wore a huge, dubbed-in ten-gallon-hat.

An arc of four cameo portraits of Stynehenge's previous wives ran around the left side of the cover. Crouching next to the scooter was a caricatured version of Hasna, her Slavic moon of a face grimacing, swastikas for eyes. She held a giant hypodermic, which tossed off several very large, dark, grainy drops of some fluid the reader could only imagine. The subscript to the cover ran: **What's Lefty Got Left?"** Inside, in a pair of short, crudely written paragraphs, the editors enlarged on the question.

Their thrust was obviously to indicate that Stynehenge was long gone, too senile and depleted to render judgments about national security. The cartoon also implied that he was subject to insidious – if undefined – influences. The swastikas meant something, although that went unexplored.

What I told Wilmot had been filtered – warped – to justify a no-holds-barred condemnation, to blind-side Lefty from the right.

Too often the tabloid expose of today morphs quickly into tomorrow's lead story, grist for the legitimate press. One thing I did know – Hasna flourishing that needle was likely to panic Murtha. The day after I returned to the Pink Streets Sonny turned up and installed motion detectors that blanketed our little property inside the fences. We kept the blinds drawn.

Until my Washington interview was over, I made sure Rick parked his Jeep Cherokee conspicuously in front – the Jeep was visible all the way to the Serpentine Drive -- and came and went decked out in battle fatigues. My aging Beemer stayed in the garage, unless I was sneaking out to confront the paperwork backing up in our law office. Then, almost always, Sonny followed closely in his khaki Chevrolet Equinox. If Sonny was right, safety for me was a matter of logistics. Murtha depended on catching people alone.

I did the brief teaser exchange in Tampa with the venerable Stewart Lorbeer. The exponent of responsible progressive thought throughout the Bay Area, Lorbeer stuck to the questions Chris Nugent had sent along. When had I visited Costa Rica? How did I happen to run into a fellow American able to divulge to me, in advance, plans by outside elements to convulse the fragile little Republic? Was it true that my drinking cohort actually *anticipated* the Honduran irregulars that sowed such havoc? Who corrupted the miners' union? What lay behind that abomination in *The Federal Investigator* about Justice Stynehenge?

Fascinated, Lorbeer drew me out. We both knew Nugent would cut the trailer to under a minute. He would know what to cut. There was a lot to work with.

The Liberation Channel aired the trailer for the first time on December 23. The response was immediate, intense. A tidal wave swamped the twitterverse. Senior government officials from State and the FBI called Nugent within an hour, demanding corroboration and in one case intimating legal action if I actually got as far as the Manhattan studio. Charging prior restraint, Nugent's attorneys backed the officials off. In and of itself, that trailer was turning into news a week before I was scheduled to appear.

CHAPTER XVI

My parents, at least, were determined that nothing and nobody was going to wreck our Christmas. That year little Carl, Linda's son by her first husband Savage Owl, was with us throughout the holy week. I say little Carl, although he would soon be almost as tall and probably ten pounds heavier than I was. Savage Owl was massive, a semiretired alligator wrestler. We all hoped Carl would inherit his size and power, if not his punishing alcoholic's disposition.

With Staniford Murtha on the loose our entire family was reduced to skulking around behind the blow-up reindeer in front of Dad's formidable residence – inevitably, the phrasing was Dad's -- like Jews in the Warsaw ghetto during the Nazi occupation. We seemed to be sighting Murtha everywhere, or thought we did.

Dad wasn't so sure. "We may have on our hands a paper tiger," Dad decided, dispensing of the last foaming trickle out of the big crystal pitcher of margaritas he had just stirred up and poured into a round of cocktail glasses for the adults. "It could just be we should have stood our ground the other day. Faced that chazar down, given him something to think about. Remember, I was carrying."

The rest of us picked up our drinks and followed Mother into the downstairs library.

"What do you think, Sonny?" Dad wanted to know. "You were on the scene."

Sonny blew reflectively into the ginger ale he was nursing. "I think it was a good idea you didn't try anything like that," Sonny began finally. "They send Murtha in to close the deal, that's his reputation. DIA has his 201 file, I had a look at it once we got back. He's hard-core pathological, outstanding at icing people with little or no warning. He knows the spooks would be stuck sometimes without him as a resource. They need him, so just about anything he gets into they'll cover up. He thinks he's double oh-seven with an incidental weight problem."

Dad chuckled.

Mother stood resting on one arm of the brocaded wing chair she favored when we were all together. She looked quite beautiful if much too pale and a little shaky, pre-Raphaelite, in her long dress. Mother took a sip of her margarita. "But if you think that," Mother said, obviously reflecting a moment first, "isn't it the quintessence of bad judgment for Michael to go ahead and bait this fellow? Appear on some TV show and tell the world that *he's* the one behind all the troubles in Puerto Rico, or Costa Rico, or wherever that terrible place is?"

Sonny looked at me. I hadn't told any of the others how I happened to meet Murtha. "My hunch," Sonny suggested, "is, we passed that point a couple of months ago. Murtha is a talker, and he got fried and shot off his mouth, and so much is already out there that once Michael spells out a few more things Mr. Murtha turns into a liability. The people he works for will take care of him."

"Eets how it is," Rick Perez attempted to affirm. Mother was trembling. "Special operations is a mother-- very tough, I did it, and in that time I see a lot of things."

We could hear Anastasia, the black woman who helped us out whenever Mother entertained, clattering up the back stairs from the kitchen below, which was at the other end of my parents' big stone Mediterranean-Revival palazzo on Brightwaters Boulevard. Anastasia set down a tray of hot crabmeat canapés. Dad wished her a wonderful holiday and gave her a hug.

There, then, it did seem all but impossible that anything could touch us. Out back, overlooking the Bay, Ten Bears and his hulking half-brother Carl were attempting to kick a soccer ball by each other while Lin Kee and her little sister Carol, Jr. and Rick and Wendy's rousing handful, young Carlos, jeered encouragement. Our tribe was filling in.

One of Dad's eccentricities was his insistence that goose be served at Christmas dinner. He thought he remembered that Dickens, in *A Christmas Carol*, compensated Bob Cratchit for so many months of abuse by granting him this one feast. My insidious sisters used to maintain that Dad secretly identified with Scrooge, and all this was some sort of neurotic expiation. In their scenario I was Tiny Tim. Still, we ate goose every Christmas.

The shadow of Murtha continued to overhang the season. Downtown I was attempting to keep everything going, although my other brother-in-law and law partner,

Buckley Glickman, now seemed even more distracted than usual. Once the main meal was behind us he stopped me while the others went back upstairs for brandy. I think my neglect of our business day-to-day, with calls from key clients going unanswered and bills languishing until I had the chance to look them over, had started to eat into Buckley's composure.

Buckley touched my shoulder. "I sure do hope this broadcast you've got on the front burner is going to settle things down," he assured me, and in a very low voice. "With you gone that ditsy clientele we pushed like mad to attract has got me flittin' all over creation. I think every nutcase ex-debutante in town had *got* to have a divorce this winter, and every one of 'em want *us* to take care of everything. There was a time when I thought, hey, wouldn't it be wonderful to rack up all those billable hours myself? I didn't have a clue, the way the stress builds up, fakin' all that sympathy nine to five." Light from a carriage lamp along the corridor was glistening through the clumps of thinning sandy hair bristling around Buckley's scalp. "Be careful what you wish for."

"One way or another, pal, this thing with Costa Rica is going to end."

"God willin' and the creek don't rise."

"You got that right," I said.

"I miss our pioneering start-up years. As I remember, my biggest worry in those days was which bus Andy Brunosovitch was going to hurl himself under next. Buses? Or was that trucks?"

"Trucks mostly," I said.

Stuffed, a few minutes later I grabbed Sonny and headed out to walk off a little of too much goose and Anastasia's cranberry and sweet potato stuffing. Most of the substantial residences along Brightwaters Boulevard amount to cunningly designed one-house gated communities, their commanding brick or paver entrances masked by plastered walls or planters overflowing giant ferns or philodendra or calla lilies or – less subtle – protected by high, sharp, black-enameled wrought-iron pickets backed up by mature hedges.

It was about to become dusk. The world was settling in after a long holiday afternoon. I didn't say anything for a couple of blocks. "The parents are worried," I said finally. "I think that adventure with Ramon was at least enough for everybody's lifetime. And now this."

Ramon was Ricky's father, who had lured Dad into investing a lot more than he should have in his hedge fund and almost took all of us down with him.

"Not that I blame you entirely for this mess," I said.

"Look at the patriotic side," Sonny said. "If this breaks right you will have helped avert a war. Saved thousands of lives, conceivably. Justified your meager existence."

"Your complacency about putting my ass on the line will be lovingly remembered." But then it came to me how often Sonny himself almost got wiped out. "OK," I said. "That was stupid."

"You've got a point." Late afternoon traffic was picking up. A lot of Lexuses and Mercedes. Arclights bolted to the highest few feet of telephone poles started blinking on. An SUV was approaching, a two-tone Ford

Explorer, black body and white cab, with very dark tinted windows. The long late-afternoon sun highlighted the silhouettes of two people in front and somebody in the back. Sonny watched the Explorer slide by and let his head angle down so he could half-whisper to me. "PJB 6673" he said. "Try and remember that."

"Because?"

"That was your drinking buddy. On the passenger side. Out reconnoitering. Probably followed you over and has been circling the area ever since."

"How could you tell? Behind all that shaded glass?"

"Head shape. On Murtha's 201 there were a couple of mug shots. He has a very distinctive skull formation – like an avocado, compressed around the top but fuller around the chops. I had a glimpse of the outline."

"Lord preserve the trained eye. Who else was in there?"

"The one you call the waiter, the tall guy, he was probably driving. Somebody else was in the back, shorter, too dark to make much out."

"This is a lot of fun," I said. "Win, lose or draw, by New Years it had better be over."

I took the non-stop to LaGuardia a couple of days later. With no idea whether any of our phones were tapped I avoided making a reservation at a Manhattan hotel. Having carried on, it was no problem to roll around the baggage carousels in the terminal and jump into the first cab in the waiting row before anybody could follow me into the swarming late-afternoon traffic. I had a hotel on the Upper West Side in mind – but no reservation – so I had the cabbie let me out several blocks to the north and trundled my luggage in and out of the mobbed sidewalks – the working day was ending – and was lucky enough to snag a single room high in the hotel.

When I rolled out of the elevator and into the room the call waiting bulb was winking. I had told Dad where I would probably put up, so I was not surprised that he was the one. He wanted me to call him right back. I did; Anastasia answered; it took Dad a little while to get to the phone.

"Jesus, I'm glad you got in touch!" Dad said. Then he didn't say anything for a number of seconds. "Listen," he said, finally. "I know you've got a lot on your plate. I think you ought to make the call on this one."

"The call on what?"

"There was—something happened. You know how your mother always likes to decide what goes into the food around here? It's a WASP tic, their agricultural heritage or some goddamn thing. There never was a produce-fondler like that woman. The thing is, Max took her marketing around two this afternoon and she..didn't...."

"Didn't what?"

"She disappeared. Max dropped her off at the Fresh Market, on Fourth Street, and drove back to park the car, and by the time he made his way around to the main door and kind of pressed on through all the leftover baby Christmas trees and net bags of pine cones and all that holiday dreck she was into it, you know? Max couldn't find her in there for a while – you know how they pile up those islands of citrus and pineapples and whathaveyou—"

"I know about that," I said. "I've been there, where

are you going with—"

"But then Max spotted Weezee in the back, by the fish counter, checking out the cod fillets and cooked shrimp – you know how your mother is obsessive on the subject of how good fish is for everybody. So Max thought, this is going to take a while. Maybe I'll go pick up a roasted chicken and some chocolate for Anastasia. So he does that—"

"Am I too young to have a stroke? Where is this headed?"

"Don't plotz," Dad said. "My point being, that by the time Max picked up his stuff and came around to see how your mother was coming he got a glimpse of two people he didn't recognize, some fellow not too tall but bulky, Max says, and a short woman, kind of hustling Weezee out the service door in the back. She was protesting but not really yelling or anything. But before Max could get there they boosted her in through the back hatch of some vehicle. Probably a truck. Max thinks the first couple of letters on the plate were PJ Something. Max says he stumbled into a pyramid of bananas but then the door closed and when he got to it and banged it open again whoever it was was long gone. With your mother."

My hand was trembling. "Did you call the cops?"

"Obviously, my first reaction. But then I got this call – a woman's voice, except tinny, some device to disguise who it was, probably. And the woman said, 'We have your wife.' Very melodramatic. 'And if you want her back your son had better not spill his stupid guts on TV to Dan Prosper. So tell him that. And keep this matter to yourself.'"

"So there it is, Michael," my father said. "What do you intend to do?"

"I don't know yet," I told my father. "I do know I will be back sometime this evening."

I had my secret cell phone with me. I called Sonny. "I guess we should have anticipated some stunt like this when Murtha drove by on Christmas," he said. "Maybe we had you too well protected, and he is getting desperate."

"But what's next. The corpse of my mother?"

"Whatever you do, if this plays out at all Murtha isn't going to let her walk. Anything and anyone she sees is going to put him at risk. The best thing for us is to figure out where Murtha had got your mother squirreled away and show up before he can get the rest doped out. I think he's improvising. What about your fifteen minutes as a cable star?"

"I don't know yet. I guess I'll get there and decide."

"Let me know your flight number. In the meantime I'll hit the warpath."

CHAPTER XVII

The Liberation Channel was downtown, high up, part of that grungy labyrinth of offices and largely abandoned old-fashioned media locations adjacent to Gracie Mansion and overlooking the East River. Our interview was scheduled for eight. Chris Nugent, a battered little camp-follower of the unending Manhattan political wars, tugged on his string tie a moment before handing me off to a tacky-looking intern-of-all-work. Chewing her gum hard and smelling of marijuana, the intern conducted me into a closet of a green room and powdered and combed me without bothering with a word. Inside, I could tell, my guts were seizing. Sonny's assurance that nothing I did or didn't do was going to help save Mother was all I had.

The studio from which this was going out live looked more like a talk radio workshop in some vocational institute than any kind of prestigious national venue. The walls were hung with political posters all the way back to the Wobblies. One almost current read: "Bipartisanship – I'll hug your elephant if you'll kiss my ass." A donkey kicking out and a pair of carmine lips illustrated the sentiment. "Don't pray in my school and I won't think in your church" ran another.

So Daniel Prosper, when he strolled in, was a surprise. The rugged trustworthy face and legendary Middle-western baritone that legitimized network news for all those years, Dan had come out politically, lending all that seasoning and fluency to convictions he must have stifled throughout four decades of corporate jets and expense-account lunches. Obviously, he still favored bespoke tailoring.

"I'm glad you came by," he greeted me, grabbing my hand with both of his. "You are performing a service, take it from this badly battered old newshound. One who is still carrying a chunk of Viet Nam around in his butt."

"My father served there," I said.

"Then you know." But Prosper obviously wasn't interested. "This will be your night in the foxhole," Prosper said. "Think we can stop a war? I'm going to wing it."

"Maybe start one," I said. Passingly, Prosper's brows curled. Two youngsters were adjusting the lights; the sound man came in to take a reading at each of our microphones before clipping them in under our lapels. Videocameras had started to whirr.

It was air time.

We sat facing each other across a blue-black formica-covered counter. Dan kept shuffling his notes. "What say we start with a few background details," he opened. He tapped the wen below his left cheekbone, something most anchors would have parted company with long ago. Even his voice sounded a little bit phlegmy with sincerity. "You are a practicing attorney, distinguished enough to have pleaded an important First Amendment case recently before the Supreme Court. You have an Ivy League background. Your father, Sylvan Landau, is a nationally acclaimed professor of economics and a celebrated writer in the field."

A camera swiveled toward me. I nodded, pinching up one corner of my mouth in a simulated smile.

"You're leading this...this regular, normal life, an established professional, and then one day you decide to take a short vacation in Costa Rica. Am I on target so far?"

"That's pretty much it," I said. "I had never been down before, and I expected to meet a friend in a day or two and do a little fishing."

"Fishing?" Dan Prosper said. "Really? Good fishing down there, especially on the Pacific side. What were you after?"

I was starting to seize up. "We were after—" I couldn't think – "bobo? Mostly it was bobo."

"Not marlin or tarpon or any of the game fish?" Prosper's glance verged on the condescending.

"I think it was too late in the season," I said.

"But then, before that, you had some time to kill in San Jose, and that was when you happened to wander into this bar and run into the fellow who involved you in that fascinating exchange that has come to light, am I correct?"

"That's pretty much it," I said. My mouth was very dry.

"And this place was just another bar in the downtown area. Nothing else going on?"

"I guess it was like most of the places in that district," I said. "There was a little gambling, I suppose. Texas Hold'em seems to have caught on down there."

"Girls?"

"I suppose," I said. This was a hard tone to sustain. "I was just, you know. Floating around. So I dropped into this place, and asked for a beer – I'm a Heinekens drinker – and pretty soon I got into a conversation with the fellow on the next stool." Prosper frowned. I had the feeling I wasn't quite bringing off my neb act.

"Did he tell you his name?"

"After a few minutes. When one of the girls joined us – you're right, there were girls, I remember now. He was already a couple of sheets to the wind, and I think he wanted to impress her. Rosa Dolorosa, I think her name was. But he said his name was Murtha. Staniford Clinton Murtha. It was easy to remember – what with the ex-president and all that."

"But why would he…?"

I was starting to loosen up. "The problem was, the girl kept coming onto me and Murtha had other ideas. So he kept trying to impress her. He told her he was a senior operations manager attached to the National Counterterrorism Center. He said he was on special assignment in Costa Rica under the auspices of the office of the vice president – Alvin Sheel. Very influential people in our country and Canada had reason to believe that in the gold fields up north there were high-priority, defense-related mineral deposits that they had a right to develop according to some treaties carried over from olden times, but the conservationist regime in San Jose refused to allow our corporations in. So he was down there to bring the whole thing to a head. All this got confused after a couple of minutes – the guy was more and more stoned, and then he started getting angry. Noise, he kept talking about making a lot of noise."

Dan Prosper regarded me solemnly. "I believe that is an intelligence term for creating a major disruption," he announced. "Did he give you any idea of what they had in mind?"

"Well – by then Murtha was pretty plowed. He mumbled something about deep-sixing some labor leader in the gold region. And then he started ranting about some Honduran bone-crushers that they had laid on to do a lot of bang and boom wherever U.S. properties down there were vulnerable."

"Well – that certainly fits," Dan Prosper agreed. "I'm sure you saw that column in *Our Republic* about how that caper worked out."

"I haven't exactly seen it," I lied. "Covers the same territory?"

"That, and more."

As I now intended, I obviously seemed more than naïve to Prosper – rattlebrained, gullible. "You may not realize it," Prosper assured me, speaking slowly so I would understand, "but everything you just said blows holes in whatever justification those professional patriots are pumping up to move into Costa Rica. Especially with the war powers decision pending. We're due for a commercial break, and after that I think I'd like to delve into certain of the *personal* consequences you've had to contend with after that serendipitous little conversation."

That last was unexpected. During my preliminary debriefing with Chris Nugent I had alluded cautiously to having encountered Murtha in Washington. I'd intended to ease past anything immediately threatening to me, expecting all that to just sort of blow away once the crisis passed. I'd forgotten Freddie Wilmot. Whatever I'd divulged to him no doubt got passed along to Nugent.

Besides, at this moment, it wasn't primarily about me. I had no idea what was happening with Mother!

Like its editorial content, many of the ads on the Liberation Channel skirted cultural correctness. One spot promoted a depilatory guaranteed to remove all hair, anywhere, for three months. "You ladies will appreciate that!" the spokesman gushed. The next spot introduced the breakthrough vibrator an established condom manufacturer was marketing – the revolutionary pulse action could be set for throb, rotate or corkscrew.

Dan Prosper sat blinking, looking a little frustrated. "Revolting, the smut peddlers we sell time to to pay the goddamned freight," he muttered to me, shielding his microphone. He was disappointed with whatever I'd said so far, I could see. He'd expected something more -- something immediate, newsworthy. Without daring to think it through, I decided to throw him what he was after.

"As we were discussing," Prosper started again, "It turned out you hadn't seen the last of your Mr. Murtha when you got back and settled down into normal living."

"That just happened," I said. "It worked out that Supreme Court Justice Grover Stynehenge is a major admirer of my dad's biographies. When he found out I was in town to argue that case in front of his court he invited me to a little dinner at his club. That's when I saw Murtha again."

"What was he doing?"

"He was—" I took a breath – "As we were getting in

off the street I saw him turning over something in an envelope to Mrs. Stynehenge – Hasna, the justice's wife."

"Ah, yes," Prosper sighed. "The latest candidate. One of the many. What did you make of that thing in that tabloid the other day – *The Federal Investigator*, wasn't it? That Nazi with the needle cartoon?"

"Probably scurrilous," I said. I was clicking in. "Those injections she gives him? From what I could tell she's just trying to keep the justice alive."

Prosper's eyes narrowed, he steepled his fingers. "That means you are unwilling to make any connection between your Mr. Murtha's having given something to Stynehenge's wife of the moment and those injections she keeps giving him and the fact that the old guy looks like death warmed over, worse every minute? Just when every progressive citizen in America is depending on him to come up with that all-important fifth vote to return the war powers to the Congress?"

I looked as concerned as possible. "I'd like to think you're wrong about that," I said. I hoped and prayed both Stynehenges were watching. "It seemed to me those two were devoted to each other." How big a spotlight did Hasna need? "I guess the proof is in the pudding, as they say. If Stynehenge holds up and gets to cast his vote, a lot of this nonsense will get forgotten soon enough. Right now I've got a lot more pressing problems with my Mr. Murtha, as you keep referring to that SOB. Can I say SOB on television?"

"This is cable. We hear a lot worse than that." Dan Prosper had started tapping on his wen with the tip of his forefinger. "These more pressing problems? Would you care to elaborate?" Prosper's exasperation with me was hard to mistake.

"Well –what the hell. OK." I felt my heart pounding in my throat. "It happens that sometime this afternoon, while I was flying up here, a stocky guy who sounds exactly like Stan Murtha and some woman kidnapped my mother, who is very sick. Then my father got a call from probably the same woman warning me not to spill my guts – that's an exact quote – to Dan Prosper on TV. I almost didn't show."

Prosper looked stunned. "Insane," he got out after a moment. "This afternoon? Your mother?"

"She is very sick," I said. "She needs her medication. I only hope anybody who sees this will help."

Prosper was still recovering. "You will – you'll bring in the FBI, I hope," he got out.

"We'll bring in the Northwest Royal Mounted Police if that will get her back," I said. "Alive."

Prosper still looked floored. "I guess we've run out of time," he got out, finally.

Once I was outside the studio Chris Nugent shook my hand, gravely. The intern came in from the hall, where she had obviously been toking, carting behind her my rollaboard. I was headed directly back to La Guardia. "Now *that's* a news break," Nugent said. "What you got into at the end." He pulled a handkerchief out and wiped what was left of the powder off my forehead. The intern was already back in the hall, working on her roach. "Interns," Nugent said. "You definitely get what you pay for."

CHAPTER XVIII

Sonny was standing waiting for me as I emerged from the tram that connected with the gates for the northern flights. We headed toward the bridge to Short-Term Parking.

"I caught the broadcast," he said as we climbed into his dusty Equinox. "Your imitation of Forrest Gump brought tears to my eyes."

"I was improvising," I said. "To start with I was scared, but then I got some ideas."

"You sure did." Sonny backed out. "Murtha as a senior operations manager in the National Counterterrorism Center? That'll get somebody's attention. They wouldn't let Stan Murtha swab out the johns in a place like that."

"That was my point. He was puffing himself up."

"What is really going to get the moose pregnant inside the Beltway is how you connected him to Alvin Sheel."

"That I didn't invent. Murtha threw that in my face just before he tried to knife me in the Metro."

"The question isn't, what's true. The question is, is what you put out there too heavy to finesse. Sheel is already bobbing and weaving a little now that the New York Attorney General is after his unpaid taxes – the word around Defense is, he's desperate for cash. Now what you're suggesting is, Sheel has been masterminding some kind of covert-action head fake that backs this country into a war. And for personal reasons -- to bail out his portfolio. Shades of Spiro Agnew. I think I'm going to weep."

We had finished winding down the ramp. I handed Sonny five dollars to pay.

"What about Mother?" I said. "I'm petrified. I figured that if I threw that in there maybe Murtha would think twice before he tried anything . He'd realize they'd go after him. The authorities."

"I wish I thought something like that." Sonny took the turnoff for the airport exit. "What you've done is turn Murtha into a luxury neither the Agency, or Sheel's hangers-on, or anybody else in that National Security nest of snakes can accommodate. I'm sure he knows this."

I'd started to breathe through my mouth. "So then he does--?"

"Murtha goes to ground. Scorched earth. Costa Rica is defunct, he can forget whatever big dollar he expected to retire on. So now he has to make sure nobody stays around who could testify against him – the threat of extradition is what spooks hitters like Murtha."

"I think I'm going to be sick," I said. "Really."

"Then he burns one of his passports to get him out of the country to someplace they like him better. He's got that Spanish, so there's a lot of choice. Paraguay. I heard he made some friends around the Ministry of the Interior down there when he was heaving labor reformers out of CIA choppers."

"So what you're saying about Mother—"

"I'm saying: We better get there first. Right after we talked I took off and headed for MacDill. I remembered how the tech sergeant who came up with that laser microphone we used in Abangares mentioned transponders. But when I got out there all he had was one battered little discontinued piece-of-crap supposedly up to date enough to operate on GPS but with LoJack backup in case Murtha stowed the Explorer inside, or we get a storm or anything like that. He says the thing incorporates the worst features of both technologies, but it ought to work. The big problem was, we have to dope out the frequency of something actually transmitting out of that Explorer, it's our only hope if we intend to track it."

"Pretty remote," I said. Rain was blowing in, big drops were spattering the windshield of the Equinox.

"You'd be surprised. Something came to me, I figured out how, so then I called your dad, and told him to alert Ricky, and meet us with anything we could use in the breaking-and-entering line. Wrecking bars, a shovel, a ladder. Any flashlights that still work, especially high-intensity. The character I share a house with in Clearwater has a lot of tools. I grabbed a bolt cutter plus one of those battery-operated drills with a carbide-disc bit. I've got my lock-pick set."

I was not feeling quite so sick.

"Then I got out here something like an hour ago and made the rounds of the car rental agencies in the terminal. I assumed that Murtha was savvy enough to have switched out the plates. Most people rent vehicles at the airport these days. That's the thing, how many Ford Explorers are the local franchisees liable to maintain at this location, right? It turned out there were three, but only one black with a white top, like the SUV we noticed on Christmas. At Budget."

"And that meant--?"

"I explained to the clerk I was with military intelligence – which technically I am – and showed him my ID and told him I was running down a homicidal deserter, crazy, liable to pile it up, who rented the Explorer. The government needed the rental people to give me the frequency for the secret transmitter they always wire into their vehicles to keep them from getting hijacked. And we had to have it pronto. Then our MPs could repossess the Explorer while it was in good shape, no harm done. The kid tried to stare me down for a couple of seconds; then he just shrugged, and read me the numbers."

"And now we – "

"Meet up with the others. In a Denny's parking area off Dale Mabry."

Serious rain was setting in, bad enough so motorists were sheltering underneath the overpasses. Dale Mabry was almost deserted. We all but skidded off the highway into the Denny's parking lot. Rick's Cherokee was parked, lights off, in one deserted corner. Beside it was a dented old pickup truck it took me a couple of seconds to realize belonged to Max.

Dad hauled himself down out of the passenger side of the truck after we pulled up. He had on the shapeless brown felt hat he kept for bad weather. "Sonny called while Max was mulching the begonias," Dad said. "He knows where we keep the gardening stuff – shovels, crowbars, a ladder – what Sonny wanted."

Max had come around the bed of the truck. Enormous, black, still in his coveralls. "Professor think I'm some kinna fool, Mike," he confided in a soft voice I had never heard before, verging on tearful. "He tellin' my business around, but what he don't wanna say is, I lost Miss Weezee. I s'posed to stick alongside her when she marketing, but do I pay attention? Where you think she gone?"

"Jesus, Max, don't beat yourself up about that," I said. "Let's concentrate on getting her back."

"But where she be?"

"Sonny has an electronic gizmo he thinks he can locate her with."

Still in the driver's seat of the Equinox, Sonny was punching numbers into a small console in his lap. "Nothing so far," he said out the open window. "Could be the rain. I think it's letting up. I liked this kind of equipment better when it was all meters and knobs and you could zero-beat the spectrum until you located the frequency."

Enrique climbed out of the Cherokee. "We got us a wet mawther-fawker," Rick said, cheerfully. Even in the glare off the hot-top I could see that he was turned out in what looked like tailored battle fatigues. A holster was visible along with a sheath-shaped pocket long enough for a bayonet. "I bat you, we gonna handle the bastards." The prospect of violence always enlivened my mercurial Cuban brother-in-law. "Just gotta find 'em, verdad?"

Sonny expressed his thin lips and drew down one brow. "I may have picked up something." There was a faint, regular pinging. "If this thing works at all, the thing to do is head north. Let's get back on the turnpike. I go first. Michel here can drive and I'll play around with this crap box of the devil."

While we were passing the turnoff for downtown Tampa another squall hit, knocking out the signal. It made sense to keep pushing north. Just before the interstate deviated and we had to decide whether to head west on U.S. 4 the torrent let up and immediately the signal came back, strong, a pounding beep, definitely indicating a swing west. But after a couple of minutes the needle on the dial jerked clockwise. "This thing is telling us," Sonny said, "to head into Ybor City."

"That makes sense. Murtha loves those fleshpots."

Tampa was all commercial; after nightfall its workaholic businessmen were known to take their neckties off and check the cash in their wallets and slink off to Ybor City. Settled largely by Cubans, before the end of the nineteenth century Ybor City had become the preeminent center for cigar-making in the United States, a rollicking sweatshop culture enlivened by the influx of greedy peddlers from Eastern Europe and succeeding generations of big-time gangsters, notably the Trafficante dynasty.

But after World War II cigar-making had died. The little community's notorious brothels along the main drag of low masonry buildings, Seventh Avenue, had given way to celebrated Mediterranean restaurants and tattoo parlors and a barber shop behind an outside fresco which emphasized the range of Afros and buzz cuts inside and a cluttered boutique that offered every curiosity from hand-painted-nude neckties to zombie skulls. Bars like Pure

Bliss and The Dirty Shame advertised Jim Beam Devil's Cut Cocktails.

As our little caravan pulled into town it was a few minutes short of midnight. Night life was still going strong. The transponder was pumping in Sonny's lap, blaring. We headed east, slowly exiting the entertainment strip. The transponder reached its loudest, then started to tone down.

Sonny told me to turn around. "Take it around this block," Sonny said. I headed north, then turned down Eighth. The transponder was all but churning, then calmed itself down again. "I think the Explorer, at least, is in *there*," Sonny said. "Take it up to the end of this block and turn around and park. Leave the other two space to park behind us. Even if Murtha posted a watch we ought to be OK."

I turned the car around and put a hand over Sonny's as he was turning the transponder off. "Look, I've been thinking. Dan Prosper probably had something. Wouldn't it make sense to pull the FBI into this? Kidnappings is what they do. I've got the office number of that agent we brought in during the Cuban thing in my cell here. Vince Hardagon. Their local headquarters are in Tampa."

"*Now* our senior legal mind faces up to reality." Sonny smiled and squeezed my shoulder. "It's basically your decision, counselor. You call a federal office at this hour, you know you'll get a computer-driven answering machine and a menu of options you can reach any time between nine and five."

"I still ought to give it a try. We've got an address, at least."

I placed the call while Sonny went to organize the others. He was right. I got a cheerful metallic voice, which said to leave a message and call back tomorrow.

The yellow block building on which we were advancing was long enough to front on Seventh Avenue and extend back all the way to Eighth. Signs front and at the side said Blitzkrieg Martial Arts and Fitness Center. There was a vehicle in the dooryard off Seventh in front of wide rusted corrugated-steel sliding doors. Windows blacked, the place had obviously been thrown together fairly recently to junk cars. All we could see in the dooryard just then was abandoned tires and a small truck jammed with rental chairs. A surrounding chain link fence was topped off by spirals of razor wire angled out.

Sonny had reached the cross-street with Max's ten-foot ladder and propped it up against the corrugated lip of the lower roof. The rain was abating now; up top I could make out several stacks, vents probably, maybe four feet wide. Over one of them was a tattered plastic tarp, wrapped on with duct tape. Sonny scrambled up the ladder and I could see his long arm against the foggy night sky in the reflection off the streetlight as he sheared off and stripped away the remnant of the tarp. We saw him hoist himself up and disappear into the vent.

"Thas how eet goes, with operations like theese *wan*," Ricky explained somberly to the rest of us. "First thing, you have to look. Maybe some kind of problems, we have to explain them that there is this thing, or that thing, before anybody move—"

In under ten minutes Sonny was making his way down, leaning backward to avoid skidding on the rain-mottled steel roof. "Your mother is in there," he announced in a heavy whisper after he swung down. "I couldn't quite see her, but once I could kind of jimmy open a corner of one of the panels of the dropped ceiling I picked up enough of the conversation to gather that they were arguing about what happens next. With her. There was a plasma TV screen on, so we have to think Murtha caught your Academy-Award performance. They seemed to be packing it in, they'll probably be out of here in an hour. The Explorer is parked next to the boxing ring."

"Who's in there?" I wanted to know.

"All your friends. Remember Audrey from your mining days? Murtha made a conquest *there*. It would be interesting to have a look at her after-action report on this assignment. The tall, boney waiter from Latvia, or wherever that was."

My father had been quiet mostly until that moment. I think he had been a little bit paralyzed thinking about Mother. "Mikey," he said now, "I have *tried* to let you go your own way, pretty largely. But you have *got* to make some new friends." The expectation that Mother was probably still alive was starting to relax him a little, loosen up his customary impulse to needle me. The worry and fatigue of the day had left him especially bug-eyed. He unzipped the top compartment of his shoulder bag, checked something, then closed it up again. "Associations are very important, Michael." Dad was running down. "I think I told you something along those lines the other day."

A sign was posted on yet another sliding rusted corrugated- steel door feet from where we stood that said GYM ENTRANCE, above a thick arrow pointing to a padlock on one edge. The bulge in one of the pockets of Sonny's rain jacket turned out to be the battery-driven drill body with the carbide wheel. Operating entirely by sound, he doffed his jacket and wrapped it around his hands to muffle the noise as he ground a groove straight through the hasp of the padlock and wrenched it and pulled it open.

Rick unsnapped his revolver holster. "So how do we do this?" Half crouched, on the balls of his feet, Ricky was primed for battle. "I think man-on-man, OK? Everybody gets some*bawdy*, like American football."

"Makes sense," Sonny said. "I assume they came in with the Explorer through the dooryard. They may not remember people can get in this way. We need to move fast. Surprise them. Rick, you grab Murtha. I'll get the waiter. Max can go locate Mrs. Landau. Sylvan can cover the rest of us in case somebody misses his assignment. These folks are bad actors, killers. Ask Mike. We've seen them in action."

The huge rusty corrugated panel slid open with a terrifying groan and we burst into the deserted gym. Just then Stan Murtha and Audrey were collapsed into butterfly chairs next to the elevated boxing ring watching a newscast and the waiter was emerging from what looked like a cluttered office off to the left. His cowlick was still loose. Rick's Smith and Wesson service revolver was already drawn.

Murtha barely looked up. His eyes were absolutely dead, registering neither fear nor alarm. He was wearing those shoot-me-first camo trousers and the canvas vest – no doubt for superstitious reasons. This operation was very high risk.

"I think you may have pushed this thing a little too far," I said, heart hammering.

"You think so? Now that you're a television personality Landau you lost touch with the everyday world, if you know what I'm gettin' at there. What did you think was gonna happen, we see those spots about how you're gonna do a tell-all on some fucking national hookup? Then when you actually spill your guts it's ninety percent bullshit. That's the real laugh."

"I think I got it right," I said. "You heard the composite version."

"Tell it to the judge."

"What are you going to do?" I got out. "Sue me for defamation of character?"

"All I'm gonna tell you is," Murtha said, "I got some very powerful friends."

"You had some very powerful friends," Sonny said from the doorway to the office. "Mike, your mother's in here. Resting on some kind of futon. She's just getting up. I'll give her a hand."

That was a mistake. The waiter had eased back into the office and now was stepping out with an assault weapon that must have been leaning against the inside door-jamb, with which he drew down on the rest of us. He gestured to Sonny to move back in.

Murtha looked at Rick. "I'm gonna need that pistol," Murtha said. "You might just get a round off if you could sight in fast enough, but by then Karlis cuts the lot of you in half. He'd have no problem with that. He's done it before." Murtha yawned. "I'll need the pistol," he repeated. "Now. Otherwise, Karlis, go ahead and take the spic out. I like our chances."

Ricky glanced up at Sonny and me, sullen. "We lookin' at a Galil AR there," Rick said. "Israeli. When he shoot that what hoppen is, she put out I donno how many slugs per second. Never gonna beat that."

"Pistol?" Murtha demanded.

Rick pitched his revolver onto the floor at Murtha's feet.

Wobbling a little, Mother made her way across the asphalt toward the rest of us. "I didn't have *any* idea this was going to turn into a *social* occasion," Mother said. She seemed very cheerful, for a kidnap victim.

Dad started toward her, then stopped. "Weezee, how are you doing? Are you holding up? I brought your prednisone."

"I could use a bath," Mother said. "Isn't this place quaint? Mirrors all along the wall, and punching bag after punching bag? And so inspirational. See all the slogans they've posted? Look." She read several aloud: "Listen to this, 'A man can fail many times, but he isn't a failure until he begins to blame somebody else,' or 'Life isn't about finding yourself, life is about creating yourself.' That's really very existential. At least that's how it strikes me. I'm hungry. Do you know who that is in that poster with the big frown and his gloves up under all the medallion girdles, or whatever they are?"

"They championship belts," Max said. "That boy Joe Frazer."

"It's *another world*," Mother said. "Everything painted red and black. Quite festive, actually."

"Arouses mankind's most primitive longings," Dad said. "Maybe a little National-Socialist, if you get right down to it. Parteitag all over again." Dad zipped open his shoulder bag. "Weez, let me give you your medicine, just in case. You do look pretty fagged. I need to know, has anybody been abusing you? Murtha or anybody?"

"Nobody has touched a hair on her frigging head," Audrey burst out. "Stan thinks she's the Queen Mother or somebody."

"That was uncalled for," Mother said. "You know, Audrey, if you insist on wearing pants suits, you should have them tailored."

"What's the percentage in getting' inta insults, Audrey?" Murtha was flushing. "It's one thing, sometimes we have to do what we have to do, but this person is quality, why make it worse?"

"You are fucked up," Audrey writhed in her sling chair. "What is this, like giving Rapunzel with the hair or somebody a terrific last meal?"

"It's because she knows she's outclassed," Murtha erupted, fighting for composure. "What am I supposeda do?" He looked up and shrugged his shoulders and at that moment Dad reached into his shoulder pack and shot the waiter with his Beretta twice, once in the shoulder and once in the right wrist. Rick wrenched the Galil out of the waiter's flopping hand. When Murtha groped for the Glock holstered behind himself, Dad picked up on the move and shot Murtha in the thigh. Max grabbed the Glock.

It was over.

CHAPTER XIX

We'd left the rusting corrugated panel ajar a couple of inches. Just then it rolled open again with its heavy, grinding noise and Special Agent in Charge Vince Hardagon and two of his street agents tromped through and took everything in. "I thought I got you off my neck a couple of years back," he greeted me. "That Cuban fiasco. But then I checked my messages an hour ago, and can you guess who is all over my bleeping Irish behind? What happened here?"

"It's a long story."

"Long or short, we're going to need an ambulance."

I told our story, at least enough of it.

"So you were thinkin', they grabbed ma, nothing we can't take care of," Hardagon said. "Bud, you're a pippin." Hardagon gestured to his fellow agents. "Runs his own vigilante squad, your full-service legal adviser. And guts galore, doesn't mind taking on the Agency.'

"Murtha isn't exactly CIA," I said. "He's some kind of independent contractor."

"Potatos, potahtoes, you sort it out. Fortunately, this is

not going to be our problem long. We cart this jerkoff to the hospital and post a guard and sometime tomorrow morning the Feds pick him up. Then he's their worry."

"But what will happen to him?" Mother wanted to know.

"My guess, they patch him up and from now on he's out of the picture. Completely. Remember those two Columbian button men—"

"The Percado brothers."

"Gone! Some shi— some dungeon in Uzbekistan, the word we got. Probably sweeping out the guest suite for Murtha here, stocking it with fresh rats. That is a very tough league to play in – they use you as an asset and you bugger things up bad enough, they don't just cut your pension. Around the Bureau the old-timers say the Agency is like what Joyce said about Ireland. It's the sow that eats its own farrow. Anybody near a disaster goes down. These other two likely to catch their lumps too."

"I thought the intelligence people just.. finessed their mistakes, Dad said. "Swept things under the rug."

"No way, this time." Hardagon eased a flask from his suitcoat pocket and took a nip and burped. "Sorry. I needed a pick-me-up," he declared, and wiped his mouth with the back of his hand. "Half the liberal marshmallows in the country probably saw Silvertongue here spell out what was really happening in Costa Rica tonight. Named names, frigged over half the bleepin' government. We got a major flap on our hands. Those turds around Langley are not going to leave the principals in this screwup running around loose so ding-dong intelligence committees in Congress can ream 'em out under the lights. No way!

Who knows how far up the ladder authorization for this kerfuffle might go? "

"Who knows?" I said.

"Weezee," Dad said, once we were heading south, "kudos. You handled yourself well. I'd have been petrified." The two were in the back seat of Sonny's Equinox.

"You know, Sylvan, in a perverse way I enjoyed the whole experience. Gave me a certain amount of pep. I'm so tied down these days."

"You may be misinterpreting Murtha. He is a very ruthless piece of work."

"I suppose," Mother said. "But the fascinating thing was, he seemed to have some kind of crush on me. It was very exhilarating, like being the best looking thing at somebody else's coming-out party. That Audrey person was beside herself."

"Well," Dad said. "After all. You know how that is. She was having turf problems. Aren't we all hostage to some extent to the imbecile between our legs?"

"It's true, Sylvan," Mother sighed in the dark.

"I imagine Mr. Murtha does have his attractions," Dad said once we came abreast of Tampa. "And I am jealous as hell. But I also think even your enormous cultivation and beauty wouldn't really have mattered at this point. Sometime tonight he intended to blow your brains out."

"Or found some amphibian to feed you to," I piped up. "Murtha has a thing for the larger reptiles."

"Comme ci," Mother said, "comme ca. I do hate being this ill, and for *so long*. Murtha isn't my type, anybody could see that, all chunky and so moody and certainly likes to throw his weight around. Definitely a bit of a palooka. But there's an *energy* there, a kind of glittery demonic presence."

"The charm wears off," I told Mother. "The palooka takes over. Be glad you caught a break."

I think Dad dozed off then. We were halfway across the Howard Frankland Causeway when Dad came to and looked around. "Sylvan," Sonny said, "you weren't that bad either. Where did you learn to shoot like that?"

"Minnesota," Dad said, and yawned. "Everybody shot. Then when I got to 'Nam there wasn't much choice. I was a platoon sergeant, and we got sent out on patrol around the base for days at a time. The Cong by then were like ghosts – they'd pop out of the foliage and you'd have maybe a second or two to take them down. Reflexes. Terrible. All those bodies. *Piles* of bodies."

"Dad got the silver star," I said.

"I wish you wouldn't bring that up," Dad said. "If I'd had any moral intuition at that age I would have been a conscientious objector. Agent Orange? Poisoning the world's jungles?

"Like this Costa Rica fiasco – the machers with the briefcases think they're going to wind up with something they can line their pockets with out of some horror show they concoct in somebody else's country. Wonderful, send the kids in, except that in the end a lot of schleppers like me never come back. Or worse." Dad exhaled, very heavily. "I think I'm very tired, " he said. "I'm lapsing into Yiddish."

After that night things quieted down in a hurry. I moved back into our place on the Pink Streets. The threat from some sort of imaginary, radicalized Costa Rica receded, even from the self-proclaimed "conservative" media. My on-air reference to Alvin Sheel's role in the attempted coup got smothered by successive news cycles, after which it was never quite picked up fully. I think I realized then for the first time how publicity-driven and ephemeral our crises have become. We have the historical memory of retarded fleas. One week our democracy cannot survive with totalitarian Communist Cuba ninety miles off the Florida coastline. Then JFK gets shot, and Castro as an issue disappears from the discussion, permanently.

After benefiting from months of astonishingly tolerant press coverage – portrayed across the media as preoccupied with his compounding tax quandry, a nightmare everyman could sympathize with -- the agile politician was able to pump up an impressive amount of widespread popular understanding. Out of respect for his party, citing mysterious family considerations, Alvin Sheel stepped down as vice-president. A pending investigation by the Senate Finance Committee was dropped. Opinion-makers on the vociferous right refused to foreclose Sheel's eventual return to presidential-level politics.

I had my fifteen minutes of national attention, consisting mostly of very short interviews on Skype and in the local television stations as one voice in the compounding debate on the role of projected American power in the emerging post-terrorist world order. *The*

Manhattan Times asked me for an op-ed piece on Central America, but never actually ran it.

When the Supreme Court finally decided Exhibitors vs. Florida, our first-amendment case, the outcome was so hedged with provisos that the new guidelines were maddeningly hard to put into practice. Like nudity, some presentation of the not-engorged genitalia was acceptable to a certain extent, mostly within an art-film context and still subject to valid community standards. We probably *had* moved the goalposts, a couple of inches. I'm not at all sure my clients among the film distributors got anything like what they were after. I never did hear from my colleagues in Los Angeles.

I have to say, the most gratifying result I got out of my season before the Supremes was a note I got from Hasna Stynehenge after the court had ruled, 5-4, that in the future even supposed "police actions" undertaken by the American military would require a Congressional declaration of war. No more shoot first, paper everything over afterwards. Justice Stynehenge himself wrote the landmark decision for the majority, another of those lucid, rigorous, at times quite whimsical essays for which the great jurist is increasingly revered.

Hasna was more straightforward. "Attorney Mike Landau," her note opened. "I know I write sometimes like not cultured person, but with us is friendship, yes? Maybe you don't think so, but my mother was teacher in Palilula, which is like suburb of Belgrade, on the Danube. She knows to write English, but with the nursing is mostly needles and bedpans, so I didn't learn too much. My best friend is spell-check.

"I just want to tell how I saw that horrible drawing in the magazine in the market, where my eyes are swastikas. How I am monster individual, which wishes to kill Grover. I think nights – some times I can not sleep – how do they think that? Then I remember how we have dinner at the club, and maybe you saw that person who give me something, so you think that person pay off her because she do something. To Grover.

Now you know, I didn't do something. I took the money because I can not help to take the money – with us after so many war we have to take the money. Like water when a person is so thirsty, like sex with teenagers. We have to take it.

"But I never hurt Grover, I rather think only about how he is. I never have no babies, so Grover is like my baby, especially when I change him. And he is extremely kind to me, nobody was ever kind like him. I think you see that, because what you say on the TV, you say, he loves her. She loves him. What you say, for me that was very beautiful. Then I can sleep, I think how I have very good life here and much better now I can sleep. Thank you.

"Maybe I think of something else, before. But when you say on TV how beautiful our love is, how can I do anything?

"When you are next time in D.C. can we get together? Or with the father? Grover thinks the father you have is awesome.

Jesus loves you,

Hasna

I wrote a polite reply. What Hasnas said – worse, what she almost said – was a lot to deal with. I'm still trying.

SNEAK PEEK AT

COMANCHE COUNTRY

BOOK THREE

THE LANDAU TRILOGY

BURTON HERSH

CHAPTER I

Dad was getting older. He'd started to resent change. "The civilization is on its uppers," he muttered to me one day while we were rounding out our traditional summer layover in Minnesota. From the bow of our rowboat he cast his fly ahead of where we were drifting. "No respect for style at all. Take cars. That Toyota SUV we rented at the airport? Looks like a big, demonic jelly bean, glowering at the road through those repulsive slanting headlights."

"And everything was better—when?"

"You probably don't remember that far back, Michael." Something was nibbling at his fly. "Before you came along. Ford made a convertible, a Thunderbird. My old man splurged, bought himself a silver-gray 1959. Wow, changed his reputation forever. And I hope I need not remind you of the Ferraris of the past." He twitched his fly rod to set the hook. "Beautiful. Standing still they were already going a hundred miles an hour." The bass he'd picked up looked about three pounds. He reeled it in a little bit absentmindedly, grabbing it as it splashed alongside the rowboat and pushed it onto the stringer. "Too many bones, but I will filet it first," Dad said.

Dad's nine year old namesake, my son Sylvan II, was crouching in front of the bait bucket at Dad's feet. Ten Bears – his Comanche name, that's what everybody called him – was tall for a ten-year-old, already almost five feet, rangy. He was growing into a long, sallow Indian face and eyes that threatened to bulge, like Dad's. The bass was sliding down the stringer toward the rippling water. It seemed to shoot a glassy, reproachful look up at Dad as it smacked the surface; Ten Bears reached down and hoisted it from under one of its gills to get a better look. "You think that hurts him?" Ten Bears asked his grandfather.

"Don't let him prong you. Hurt? Not much," Dad said. "Cartilage mostly, inside his lower jaw."

"But then when we get him back to camp?"

"Air. They can't breathe air. Although once you start cutting them up—" Dad stopped. He pulled the stringer back up and slid the bass off. It flipped once and churned toward the depths. "I guess it's catch-and-release on this trip," Dad said.

Between Dad and Ten Bears very little needed to be said. Ten Bears' mother, my intuitive wife Linda, is a retired powwow dancer and a full-blooded Comanche. Like her warrior of a brother Sonny she seems to depend most of the time on implication. A slightly elevated eyebrow, the suggestion of a twitch at the corner of a mouth – more than enough. I suspect a couple of centuries on horseback alternately hiding from and pillaging the invading whites must have inculcated that Native American ability to gauge nature moment to moment and survive. And it may be that somebody like my academic, scientific father, after a lifetime of groping after clues as to how the hidden economic universe tips itself off – Dad himself probably falls back most of the time on hints and portents. Pushing seventy now, utterly bald except for the side wisps and conspicuously grizzled, a hero in Viet Nam, he still has plenty of that case-hardened Hebrew-American *stuss*, a Yiddishism he himself likes to throw out. The tough, wry old codger who's managed to handle everything and survive everything. Beyond race now, beyond social class. Probably not so far from the Stone-Age mind.

And that could be why Dad and Ten Bears grocked.

Me, I guess I'm representative of the respectable – read *bourgeois*, if you have to – mid -- generation of the illustrious Landau line: good family man, moderate in my politics, reasonably successful attorney. To join our fishing ritual my outspoken youngster Ten Bears had flown up a day before from Oklahoma City, the culmination of a week with his Uncle Sonny on the Comanche reservation in Lawton. Sonny was a special-assignment scout with the 113 Cavalry. Semester by semester he was picking up a Ph.D in environmental sciences at the University of Oklahoma. He was a lanky, rawboned professional soldier in the second half of his twenty-year hitch with a quietly decisive personality that came alive once in a while as outrageous teasing – a subversive streak I was starting to see more and more of these days in Ten Bears. Sonny and his nephew looked a lot alike, and they got along.

"What did you make of the reservation this time?" Dad asked Ten Bears. Dad crouched to fish up a minnow from the bait can to impale on the hook of the rod and reel he had brought for Ten Bears. Then Dad thought better of that. Probably minnows had souls too. "Here, I will pinch a couple of weights on the line behind this bassarino and you can troll while we cast," Dad told Ten Bears. "You haven't told us what you ran into around Lawton." From what I'd heard, Lawton was a strip-mall-type crossroads town in southern Oklahoma near the Texas border adjacent to Fort Sill. It survives these days as the de-facto capital of the Comanche Nation.

"Hot," Ten Bears said. "Hotter than a witch's tit."

"Which witch are we talking about?" Dad demanded. "The witch of Endor or the Wicked Witch of the West?"

That was too much for Ten Bears. "I don't know." Ten Bears shrugged. "That's just something the guys say." Ten Bears watched his line go out. "No rain up there for four years. Everything is like, *brown*! Sonny took me to this wildlife refuge and I saw a buffalo eat a cactus. Big old barrel cactus Sonny said it was. Just chomped it down in these big mothering bites. *Huge* bites. I guess it was thirsty."

"*Down* there," I said. "We're in Minnesota now." The Landau family was based in Florida, St. Petersburg. The rest of the country was up there to Ten Bears.

"We had a earthquake," Ten Bears announced. "They knew it was coming but then it was a lot worse than they said. We got to hide out in the gun room of where grandpa works." My wife's father, Sam, is the Chief of Police for the Indian community in Lawton. "Talk about shook up, a couple of shotguns came off a wall and one of 'em went off and was grandpa pissed! Tasers, too. Sonny said it was worst than a tornado."

A few hours later, regrouping at the lodge, I got a telephone call from Sonny, who had stayed behind to look in on his aging mother Sakwa in Lawton. Also my mother-in-law, Sakwa was a throwback, an ancient, wizened tribal healer. Sakwa was holding up, Sonny reported, but there were…local problems he kept running into. Maybe I could stop off there on our way back from Minnesota. So he could show me what he had in mind. The tribe had its own lawyer, but tribal politics could get loose easier than I might think these days, and Sonny had a hunch that some of the special-interest sharpshooters around Lawton that summer were leaning on the guy. Maybe somebody from outside, like me, could clear things up. An outside lawyer. Like me.

Sonny wasn't a person it was easy to say no to. Along with which, our family owed him a lot. I said I'd see what I could do about our return reservations. Ten Bears stayed on with Dad, and I got the last seat on the only direct flight and carried off in Oklahoma City on Monday. Sonny met me at the gate. He tossed my carry-on into the back of the big, faded Chevy Equinox he'd bought once its lease ran out and didn't say anything until we were headed south on Route 44, the H. E. Bailey Turnpike.

I'd never seen anyplace so flat or so scorched-looking. Even through the labored growl of the aging crossover's air conditioning there was no mistaking the unrelenting keening of the wind, a spoiling, constant pressure of heat feeding through day and night from Texas and wasting the cracked prairie for miles and miles in every direction. Lean cattle grazed, Holstein and the occasional battered Jersey, foraging along the sagging barbed wire beneath dead-looking elms and mesquite and whatever weeds survived in the last of the runoff mud. Ten Bears was right, everything was a faded brown, even the long rows of Fort Sill's squared-off dependent housing quarters, like faces constructed of children's blocks with blank windows for sightless eyes.

"Four years," Sonny muttered after a while, reading my mind. "Barely a sprinkle. They irrigated for a while out of the shallower aquifers, but now they've started to go. The ones that aren't contaminated."

"Isn't that the pattern here? Surviving in the dust bowl?"

"Not like this. This is global warming." Sonny's eyes had started to narrow. "Why us, every time?" he burst out. "Need hides and skins? Massacre the buffalo! Let the noble savage starve. Promise the constituents forty acres and a mule? Run the red man off, he could use a long walk. Classical!"

This wasn't like Sonny, who certainly wasn't a whiner. Off in the distance to the west, shimmering in the heat, was the ridge line of what looked like low, chalky mountains. I gestured. "What are those?"

"The Wichitas. Something the glaciers left. Our elders used to think the spirits of our dead would wind up haunting those sacred rock piles. Very consecrated ground."

Sonny kept to himself for a few minutes while we paid a toll and got back up to speed again. He wasn't through. "What frosts my assimilated nuts," he broke out suddenly, "is the way the *tribe* here seems to be going along with the way everything is breaking down. I dropped in on the last Council meeting, and the drought came up, and all the elders just sat there. The tornadoes blow through, and now an earthquake every month, and the people here just take it!"

"What are the choices?"

"What are the choices?" Sonny's eyes were narrowing, in profile the dark shiny hidelike skin was pulling tighter across his cheekbones, accentuating the hump in his nose. "Don't sell, say no. Every time some greaseball from one of the drilling outfits comes through and pitches a ten-thousand-dollar lease option to one of our people there isn't even a negotiation. Like – there's one old rummy, Peter Red Elk. Just down the road from Ma, rotting away in one of those decomposing shotgun shacks with a couple of his grandchildren. Took the option two years ago, and overnight the rig went in, and six months later the lot of them were brushing their teeth with methane and there was a permanent oil slick making a ring inside his clawfooted old bathtub. One of the youngsters is already taking radiation for lymphoma. And needless to say, down where the boundary adjoins Ma's place, the drilling equipment is hammering away twenty hours a day."

"What you're talking about—"

"I'm talking about fracking. Motherfucking *Fracking*! The salvation of the Republic and no doubt what snaps our string around here."

"*Mother*fucking? Ph.D candidate like you?" Sonny was frowning. "OK, what should the locals be doing?"

"Do? Start making the connection. Stop selling their mineral rights, for one thing."

"When did this start, you bellyaching like this?"

Sonny snorted. "I must be softening up. I know what you're getting at, Mike. It's always a mistake to educate the aborigines."

We exited the turnpike and turned off almost immediately into a cluster of franchise motels. "I reserved a double room at the Holiday Inn," Sonny remarked as we swung up into a parking area adjacent to the lobby. "From our window you can see everybody coming or going."

"That doesn't sound good."

"Never too careful. Anyhow, I had been putting up all last week at my father's, so to speak. He's entitled to one of the big bungalows on the edge of the Comanche Tribal Complex, eight or ten miles out of town to the north. So that's not that convenient. Then there's his current live-in, Abeelia. Background pretty much law enforcement. She signed on with Sam originally as deputy chief at the headquarters. But while she was TDY finishing up her training around D.C. somebody got her involved in environmental sciences at American University and man did she get religion, big time. She came back all worked up about meltdown and the rest, so Sam arranged for her to double up running the Comanche Nation Environmental Center, which was just getting funded.

"When I first met her she was your heavy-set

hard-bitten matter-of-fact policewoman- type lady. Rarely an extra word. But then she found out I've been picking up credits in environmental studies. Right away whenever I'm in town I'm her sounding board. She keeps me up for hours after Sam turns in moaning about the degradation of the polar icecaps."

"And you can't handle that?"

"She's carrying it way too far. We need to save the planet together, I'm her secret soul mate. The other day when Sam was out all of a sudden she bounced out of the bathroom on me wearing nothing but her gun belt and a couple of holstered revolvers. Hanging very low, on every level. Complete surprise! Where was *that* supposed to go? Hard to pretend I didn't notice. I all but jumped out a window."

"That's why you got me down here? To protect your virtue?"

"Maybe that is a factor. Along with the legal advice."

Part of the problem, Sonny told me over dinner, was the dissolution of the Comanche identity. There was a lot of intermarriage, even among the tribes, and limitations and prerogatives that went back to the Grant administration had left the remnants confused about their rights and privileges.

This was an agony for the Comanches in particular, who continued to pump themselves up as descendants of "The Lords of the Plains," the white man's nightmare who pushed the conquistadors back into Mexico and overwhelmed whole garrisons of federal troopers and gang-raped any woman who survived in the stockades before scalping her and butchering her infants. Back the palefaces off! Indomitable, disciplined enough to survive if it came to that by licking the moisture out of the steaming entrails of their exhausted horses. And here they languished, their demoralized descendants, helpless in the modern world, as often as not sullen wards of a condescending government. Alcohol and drug victims, reduced in too many cases to welfare handouts and the bickered-over annual distribution from their monopoly on casinos and smoke shops. Their language was dying out, and tales of the stringy barrel-chested terrors of the prairies slung along one side of their mustangs, each taking out a half-dozen Union troopers with arrows before the terrified bluecoats could tamp the powder into their muskets – all that was legend, outworn generations earlier.

"We make some attempt to keep it going, culturally, at least," Sonny wound down. "We promote the hell out of our Code-Talkers during World War Two. But commercial America today is apparently too much for us. What little we have, we can't wait to sell out."

We were having ribs, which arrived. "And what should I do?" I asked.

"We need to start with the documents. The way it's developed, there really isn't a 'reservation' around here anybody could claim any kind of effective title to. Our people have sold off so much of their property the whole county is checkerboarded. Whites-Indians, Indians-Whites, with one set of regulations for our people and another for legitimate citizens around here. Sam's job is to keep the lid on whenever a Comanche is involved. Whenever one Indian cuts another one, Sam is supposed to step in and patch up the situation. Where whites are involved the civil authorities take over. It's law-enforcement apartheid."

"And all that is part of the legal framework?"

"From what I can tell, Mike, there really isn't that much legislative framework to go by. With fracking turning into a big-bucks enterprise around here we've got a major-league rights grab on our hands, and the powers in Oklahoma City are attempting to bulldoze *us*. With our help. Our legal claims supposedly go back to the Medicine Lodge Treaty all the southeastern chiefs signed when Andrew Johnson was president, the eighteen-sixties. We agreed to let the railroad through and confine our people to maybe three million acres of territory down here, where we would maybe take up farming and do whatever we were told. Washington -- the utterly corrupt Bureau of Indian Affairs -- was expected to maintain agency outposts to provide the survivors food and supplies. This would be the Native American homeland. It was always assumed that whatever else was involved – water, mineral rights – went to us.

"At least that's what *we* assumed. It turned out what little food we got was worthless – rancid bacon and salt pork . A few of the Eastern tribes fooled around with farming, but most of our braves were still too restless and bloodthirsty to just give up and watch the buffalo herds get exterminated by Yankees in tuxedos blasting away above the railings of their cabooses . Mountains of dead buffalo, the end of our way of life. And we were expected to stay drunk and do whatever we were told, so pretty soon we were back to raiding the neighbors to keep our skill-set intact.

"But we always assumed we owned whatever they let us keep. Except now the State of Oklahoma has started to tell us we probably don't have any justifiable claim even on the water and mineral rights under what's left of our own properties. Sell when you get the chance, eminent domain is on the way. Wildcatters operating in the name of the corporations are pushing the politicians to let them jump in and pump those carcinogens by the tank-car-load into our water tables and go for the oil and gas."

I finished the last of my ribs. "Those are the documents you were talking to me about on the phone," I said.

"Whatever you can find," Sonny said.

"You realize I'm licensed to practice only in the State of Florida. Didn't you say the tribe had its own legal representation?"

"From what I can tell the people we use have been candyassing around this issue for at least two years. It could be they're already bought and paid for. We need basic information. A contract is a contract. Let's see what you turn up. Go spend a day in the Bureau of Records downtown and see if you can get your hands on some of those agreements the drillers have been writing with these saps around here. If the old treaties carry over at all, a lot of these hit-and-run arrangements could very well be invalid. We're looking for something to go to court with, maybe get injunctions. I'll have Sam call ahead and make sure you get in."

"Why am I always expendable?" I muttered. "I haven't looked forward to one of your assignments this much since you planted me in that whorehouse in Costa Rica."

"You'll like this project a lot more," Sonny said. "You make much better decisions with your pants on."

There was a rudimentary law library in an alcove of the municipal courthouse in Lawton, source books and a surprisingly comprehensive bank of computers with specialized internet connections. I got there early the next morning and kept after the apprehensive old clerk of courts about where to look until he ushered me into the library itself at ten. I was interested in whether any of the treaty regulations that had accumulated over the decades might have any application to contemporary property law. The histories that were available made it only too clear that whatever the U.S. Government proposed in 1867 had been ratcheted down in successive acts of Congress that depended on an expansive interpretation of "plenary rights." There had been crippling hesitations on all sides all along. The original provisions at Medicine Lodge were signed for the Comanches by Chief Parry-wah-say-men – Ten Bears! -- , who demanded to know "...why do you ask us to leave the rivers and the sun and the wind and live in houses? Do not ask us to give up the buffalo for the sheep."

The tribe itself refused to ratify. After twenty years Congress superseded the original terms with provisions in the Dawes Act which provided for homesteads – 160 acres was the recommended allotment – parceled out to individual households rather than even pretending go along with the pretense of common tribal holdings. Domesticate the savages, teach them the responsibilities of ownership!

Five minutes after the boom in shale oil was underway the wildcatters started moving in. As early as 1985 lawsuits were starting to roil the local courts over whether the purchase of mineral rights by one of the fast-moving "exploration companies" carried with it automatic access to unlimited supplies of "groundwater." A great deal of groundwater was going to be required. Laden with industrial chemicals the drillers refused to identify, hydraulic fracturing mandated that this mysterious if foul-smelling "brine," and in stupefying quantities, was to be forced under tremendous pressure back into deep shafts to dissolve minerals and kill bacteria and help break open the veins through which the hydrocarbons could be pumped to ground level. Apart from the inevitable contamination of local drinking water, the process surfaced heavy concentrations of radioactive chemicals and salt, which the drillers routinely pushed back into very deep supporting shafts scattered around the sites. But the earth itself often seemed to struggle to regurgitate this very heavy mixture of unnamed chemicals the drillers kept force-feeding it. Earthquakes were more and more common around the region, and of gathering intensity.

Sonny filled me in on the politics at lunch. Until the Bush/Cheney era, technicians on the Oklahoma Water Resources Board had attempted to limit the scale and pollution of the ever-more-aggressive drillers. But with a Tea-party-oriented government in the state capital, the tendency was to go along with whatever the hard-pressing oil men and their lobbyists kept demanding. In and around Lawton the proliferation of rigs was starting to dot the landscape. Especially to the west, punctuating the foothills that adjoined the wildlife refuge leading into the Wichita Mountains just north of Cache.

By now it seemed to Sonny that not only was some overworked drilling rig churning away against the pewter sky around every second bend, but behind each one lurked the outline of enormous rectangular galvanized vats, stories high, fed by a sprawl of hoses each a foot in diameter. The whine they made pulling through and recycling the obnoxious slurry was audible from the road. Even driving by, the soil blackened by the seepage and overflow from this constant tide of chemicals stank, badly.

While I was nosing around the courthouse, Sonny had arranged for Sam to call ahead and get me into the bureau of records to look over the contracts between the landowners and the exploration companies. Sonny dropped me off, but I noticed him parking around the corner. Deeds and contracts were on file upstairs. Guarding the door to the archives in shirtsleeves, behind a vast desk, sat a stumpy, moonfaced custodian with a pencil moustache and a sty inflaming his left eye. I explained that I was there on an errand for Chief of Police Ketahtoh Oscola – Sam's Anglo name, more serviceable than the original Ten Bears – and that I gathered that Sam had called ahead. The custodian grumbled that he had heard something about that and rose, heavily.

"We got electronic records, back ourselves up and the rest of the drill," the custodian said, and itched his eye with a knuckle. "People still want dupes, paper, you tell me why." He opened his hands toward the filing cabinets. "Be my guest, bottom two drawers."

"Where are the copying machines?"

"You after copies? The word I got, nobody mentioned copies. That's not so easy, we got regulations too." We stood there looking at each other. "When you get all done, you bring whatever you got to me. We'll work out copies."

"Fair enough." I watched the little custodian, hands balled, marching out the records room door. Just as he left he was starting to fish for a cell phone. He wasn't going to give me a lot of time. Squatting before the first of the drawers I lifted out a dozen or so of the lease agreements and splayed them across a work table. Seven, I saw, were issued by the same driller, Coyote Creek Development. Headquartered in Cleveland. Every one of them was drafted in pretty much identical boilerplate, the worst of it buried in footnotes or intentionally garbled extremely fine print.

The landowner agreed to relinquish, in perpetuity, all rights and claims to subsurface assets, mineral and otherwise, in liquid or solid state. The development corporation would be authorized to introduce equipment of any size, weight or configuration to effect unlimited recovery of such assets. The landowner would waive any future claim or legal action against the Coyote Creek Development Corporation in the event of any and all alleged damages or lawsuits and/or threatened recourse to any relevant state or federal agencies arising out of the anticipated extraction process. The one-time payment was stipulated in each case, and varied remarkably, according to the arrangement struck.

Environmental law is not my specialty, but I could spot four or five clauses in any of these agreements that had to be in unembarrassed violation of settled federal law, especially the environmental protection guidelines. The custodian had struck me as iffy, disapproving, so I took out my cell phone and attempted to photograph relevant sections in four or five leases. I had finished with four when a siren in the building went off; the custodian rushed in.

"Smoke alarm," he husked out. "We gotta clear the place!"

I grabbed my briefcase. Smoke floated along the corridor. The burly little custodian was immediately behind me, all but prodding an elbow into my back as he picked at his eye. I thought I took in flames licking up out of something but the custodian moved me along and out to the landing above the central staircase. "We go down there!" the custodian rumbled behind me. "Nobody gets to use the elevator, that's your state regulations."

Passers-by were gathering on the street. I made my way around the block toward Sonny's Equinox. He had settled in behind the wheel. "I didn't get far," I told him. "Some kind of fire."

"Did you get anything?"

"I got the gist of most of the contracts I saw. I

tried to photograph...three, maybe. With my cell phone."

"You done good. Maybe ten minutes after you showed up a couple of greasers in hip-huggers and very pointy snakeskin boots showed up in back and let themselves in by the sub-basement. Shoulder-length hair, dramatic, straight out of some slasher flick. The one jet black, the other almost pink it was so white. Offsetting -- pepper and salt."

"Father and son, would you think?"

" No, no, no. It's that *forjido* look these hoods were after. Something to petrify the clientele. Probably working the day's collections, and now they get this call. Mid-level cartel muscle, ten to one Mexican. I edged in right behind the two of them once they were coming off the top of the service stairs. By then they were dumping lighter fluid into a couple of waste baskets before they flipped in matches."

"Why?"

"Why? They needed you out of there. A lot of power is moving in around this corner of the dust bowl right now, a lot of very big money itching to be made. You looked like trouble. Wrong questions. Contracts? They've got the locals wired, and probably somebody tipped somebody off. You'd better watch your ass from now on."

"Me? How about you?"

"Me? Get serious, what should I worry about? Nobody saw *me*." Sonny grinned his punishing grin. The siren from a fire truck was wailing, getting closer.

Back at the Holiday Inn there was a side room called the Courtesy Business Office where guests could catch up with their e-mail. I closed the door, and after a few tries got into my own messages. A few minutes later I was able to download the gallery section of my cell phone into the My Pictures folder of My Documents. Then I printed out everything I had attempted to photograph in the Bureau of Records. Everything came out fuzzy, but it was all legible. After that I deleted everything. Why leave evidence?

Sonny looked pleased enough when I turned over my printouts to him at dinner. "My question is," I opened, "if everything is as locked up around here as you say it is, what good will any of this do?"

"It's mostly a question of word getting out of town to the right people," Sonny said. "I think I mentioned her, the tribe has its own head of environmental affairs, the office is in a cabin way out beyond Bingo Road on the other side of the Tribal Complex. Remember, Sam's squeeze at the moment, Abeelia? Until now she's been mostly about air quality – you should hear her on kids and asthma – but now the city water has started to smell, and she's discouraging the tribal members from drinking it. Lonely voice, with Outreach Development all over the place buying up rights and telling the homeowners you'd better jump on board this big fracking boat while you can still gobble up your share of whatever payout's been budgeted – well, you know how it is, people get hysterical with greed. And of course the state keeps brushing the tribes off...."

"So – how can your friend help?"

"Abeelia's not my friend! She's my dad's friend." Sonny's brows knit. "I think I mentioned, she took some courses at American University and she still has her buddies around Washington. Bush II starved out the Environmental Protection Agency, but now they're getting enforcement staff back, and Abeelia went to school with a couple of the technical guys starting to make rank again. It always takes paper, documentation, to light a fire under the federal bureaucracy. Let's see how it plays -- *you* may just have come up with enough hanky-panky to authorize an investigation. We can only hope whatever you stole for us violates federal law."

"Now I'm a thief? I thought I was a patriot."

"We'll let the courts decide. Last refuge of a scoundrel, right?"

Look for other titles in the Landau Trilogy:

THE HEDGE FUND
WET WORK

Acknowledgements

A number of literary people have now read and responded to The Hedge Fund. Let me now indicate a few whose comments seemed most germane and useful. First – he deserves a paragraph of his own – I want to thank the inimitable George Pequignot for his discerning and unmatched help with our publishing ventures over what is now decades. An original and powerful writer himself, his legerdemain all around the universe of computer composition and printing details has been genuinely indispensable.

Several individuals were especially useful while I was pulling together the background information that fed this book. Francis Sing, herself for years a prominent Comanche pow-wow dancer, sparked a lot of what animated my narrative. Professor Carolyn Johnston of Eckerd College and Chief Billy Cypress put me on the trail of a great deal of Native American sociology, which I used freely. I checked out and expanded or eliminated many of the financial details that drive this story with Michael Miller, a very seasoned banking and market expert. Ray Hinz, the impresario of Haslam's internationally famous bookstore, supplied a lot of the ballistic and intelligence background I needed from time to time.

I actually read quite widely into the literature of the Native American experience. Two books come to mind among the many. *The Seminole and Miccosukee Tribes of Southern Florida* by Patsy West was very helpful. I couldn't have done without *Sanapia, Comanche Medicine Woman* by David E. Jones.

A number of friends, several well established literary personalities, have been kind enough to read and respond to my text. They include Kay and Mike Barnes, Charles Gaines, Hunter Hague, David Kranes, Ron Satlof, James Wightman. Many thanks, much appreciated.

This redesigned edition of *The Landau Trilogy* owes more than I could ever express to the design talents, computer expertise and seemingly endless patience of Shayne Leighton, the sparkplug of The Parliament House & Parliament House Book Design, who has guided this major effort at digital publication in and out of the shoals of today's technical jungle. For this I remain grateful -- more than grateful. Thanks!

Burton Hersh, November 2013

Made in the USA
Columbia, SC
05 July 2024